T0116901

A Visitor In Time

Sam I Hamm

iUniverse, Inc.
Bloomington

A Visitor In Time

iUniverse books may be ordered through booksellers or by contacting:

iUniverse
1663 Liberty Drive
Bloomington, IN 47403
www.iuniverse.com
1-800-Authors (1-800-288-4677)

ISBN: 978-1-4502-9793-6 (sc)
ISBN: 978-1-4502-9794-3 (ebook)

Printed in the United States of America

iUniverse rev. date: 8/19/2011

The author also wishes to acknowledge people whose friendship, love and inspiration have helped along the way. Firstly, to all Hamm family members, including Edward H. Hamm, Jr., executive producer of the film "The Box" starring Cameron Diaz. Also, to Doug Green, author of the poignant book No Wife, No Kids, No Plan--a must read for anyone downsized from Wall Street in the 'Zeros. And, to Reverend Daniel De Gugliemo--producer and interviewer at Cambridge Community Television (CCTV) and creator of the Treaty of Respect for Native Americans. My hats off to you, Danny, for your hard work in honor of indigenous peoples of the Western Hemisphere! Also, to my entertainment lawyers Elaine M. Rogers, Esq. of Meister, Seelig and Fein, LLP and Mark A. Fischer, Esq. Of Duane Morris, LLP. And to Alberteen Anderson, Deputy Director of Special Events, Government and Community Relations of The New York City Transit Authority who first exposed me to screenplays, and to New York City Detective Ken "Biff" Bifferelli, the greatest non-acting actor ever! Also, to Dr. Brian Taggert, screenwriting professor at UCLA Extension and screenwriter of "Adam-12" and "Emergency!" and "V" fame, my first screenwriting professor, for his belief in me, and to Dr. Susan Steinberg, PhD, my Harvard screenwriting professor under whose direction this screenplay was completed. As well, to Tom Jenks, Senior Acquisitions Editor for Scribner Publications and Professor of English at UC Davis and Editor of The Narrative literary magazine, my literary editor. Many thanks, Tom, for taking me on as a client and believing in me all these years! And to three authors: Mrs. Anne Seymour, and the Jerry Kamstra/David Jew team, authors of the soon-to-be-published book The Golden Serpent about the 1978 Golden Dragon/Triad gang massacre in San Francisco's Chinatown. Can't wait to read it, boys! Finally, to special friends along the way: Duke University's Joel Fleishman and Professor Ole Holsti, the LSE's Dr. Michael Hodges, "Harmonica" Tom Boland of the rock'n'roll band The Ethnix, Marine Corps marine Perri "The Hobo" Rlickmann, Darryl Leeland Sanderson, Daniel Senecal, Emilie Griffin, Todd Kevin Smith, Tomas "Tomasito" Regalado, Jimmy Zanze, Alan Dabrowski of Shane Toothpaste of Chicago, Paul Berry of Harvard Square's Grafton Street, Dr. Jeffrey Gilbert, Dr. Robert Ananow, Charles Flynn, and Johnathon "Jay" Giordano. Also, to the following Harvard Square musicians: the little strummer boy--Kevin So--Mary Lou Lord, and Danielle Miraglia. Lastly, to two prominent Nostradamus scholars: John Hogue, who named Nostradamus' Third Anti-Christ "Baal Hammon" with an anagram of "Mabus," and to Oxford University Nostradamus scholar Erika Cheetham.

Finally, to Winona, whose role as Blanca Trueba in "The House of the Spirits" was the inspiration for this screenplay's character Gabriella Torres de la Dalton; to Ben, whose role in "Good Will Hunting" as Chuckie was the inspiration for the character Sam I Hamm; and to Robin, whose role as Sean in "Good Will Hunting" was the inspiration for Einstein herein.

This book is dedicated to the Einstein family, and to science and science fiction lovers around the world.

FADE IN:

INT. SAM I HAMM'S BEDROOM, HOUSE, DANA STREET, CAMBRIDGE, MA (1998) -- NIGHT

SAM I HAMM sits alone at the desk in his sizeable room. On the bedroom walls are Edward Hopper and Norman Rockwell posters, as well as Hiroshige and Hokusai Japanese woodblock print posters. In front of him is a binder filled with sheets of paper. He turns each page slowly, then takes off his glasses and rubs his eyes. GABRIELLA TORRES DE LA DALTON peers into the room's doorway, then walks in and puts her arms around his shoulders and kisses him superficially on the cheek.

                    GABRIELLA
          How goes things, my little
          antichrist?

                    SAM
          Not so good.
               (beat; gesturing to
               binder)
          John Hogue in his book <u>Nostradamus</u>:
          <u>The New Revelations</u> names the
          antichrist "Baal Hammon."

                    GABRIELLA
          Forty-eight defined quatrains.

                    SAM
          That's right. And I'm stuck.

INT. OVAL OFFICE, WHITE HOUSE, WASHINGTON, DC (1998) -- DAY

PRESIDENT CLINTON sits behind his desk with Secretary of State HARVEY KISSMAN on the other side. On the speaker phone is the VOICE of ANTHONY ROBBINS.

                    CLINTON
Can't believe it. We've done
everything for Sam I Hamm.
I've had speeches at San
Francisco's Krissy Field because he
lived in the Marina District, my
daughter's attending Stanford
because San Francisco was supposed
to be the epicenter of the year
2000. We've bugged his phone,
computer and his V.W. microbus.
All to no avail. Now he's at the
John F. Kennedy School of
Government at Harvard. Tell me,
Tony, what on earth do we do now?

                    ROBBINS (V.O.)
Sam needs a mentor. Needs someone
who can help him write a book. You
need someone in the literary world
or entertainment industry to work
with him.

                    CLINTON
Harvey, any ideas?

                    KISSMAN
Woody Allen and Tom Wolfe are
obvious choices. Both are
unquestionably accomplished.
However, each is excruciatingly
busy, and likely will not help even
if Hamm is Nostradamus' Third
Antichrist. Helping him would be
an act of charity, and they want to
make money on their own products.

                    CLINTON
Tony, how fast can a book be
written?

                    ROBBINS (V.O.)
I wrote Awaken the Giant Within in
a month. Had to. One of my
business partners ran off to Rio
with eight hundred thousand dollars
when my net worth was only one
point two million. If I hadn't
written that book in a month, I'd
otherwise have had to declare
bankruptcy. Look, what Sam needs
is someone who's smart who has time
on his or her hands.

                    CLINTON
Harvey, who fits that profile?

Kissman looks down at his lap, thinking for a long beat, and
then looks up.

                    KISSMAN
Between you and me, Mr. President,
I am on Majestic Twelve, the body
responsible for overseeing the
U.F.O. phenomenon. From Nineteen
Seventy-three to Nineteen Eighty-
three there was a time travel
experiment conducted by John von
Neumann of the Manhattan Project
and Al Bielek, Harvard, Nineteen
Thirty-six, who joined forces with
U.F.O.s to time travel. The C.I.A.
oversaw the project, which was
named Phase Three of the Phoenix
Project. It continues to run today
as Phase Four.

                    CLINTON
    What're you getting at?

                    KISSMAN
    Albert Einstein fits the profile of
    the type of person required to help
    Hamm. All he did all day at the
    Institute for Advanced Study at
    Princeton was think. His was just
    about the greatest mind this world
    has ever known.

                    CLINTON
    So you're saying we use Phase Four
    of the Phoenix Project to go get
    Einstein, huh?

                    KISSMAN
    Precisely, Mr. President. Bring
    him forward in time from a year
    just after World War Two at a time
    when he was becoming a prominent
    humanitarian to today. Hamm and he
    could compare life on Earth after
    World War Two to today, around the
    turn of the millennium. Einstein
    wrote a great many books, and spent
    his entire life engaged in thought.

                   ROBBINS (V.O.)
    Who better than that? Besides,
    with the times being so politically
    correct and tranquil, he's going to
    need someone like that to inspire
    thought.

                    CLINTON
    Then Einstein it is. We'll call
    this, uh...Project Freeeh Love,

named after F.B.I. Director Louis
Freeh.

                    KISSMAN
Hoover back in the 'Forties can't
hear a word of this. He will
attempt to have Einstein deported
should he find out what is being
done. Will wonder what the near
Twenty-first Century needs with a
communist.

                    CLINTON
Agreed. We'll have a book yet!

INT. EINSTEIN'S OFFICE, INSTITUTE FOR ADVANCED STUDY,
PRINCETON UNIVERSITY, PRINCETON, NJ (1948) -- DAY

Einstein is hunched over his desk poring over papers, using
a pencil to make corrections and add to equations. There's a
KNOCK on the door.

                    EINSTEIN
     Enter!

CARL BAXTER, a white male Central Intelligence Agency agent
in his mid fifties, enters.

                    BAXTER
     Professor Einstein, I'm Agent Carl
     Baxter, Central Intelligence
     Agency.

Einstein peers over at him a beat: what does the Federal
Government want <u>now</u>--is this one of Hoover's boys here to
harass him?

                    BAXTER (CONT'D)
I don't quite know how to explain
this, but you're needed in the year
Nineteen Ninety-eight. We need you
to help Nostradamus' Third
Antichrist write a novel.
We want him to be famous by the
year Two Thousand, and I have
orders from President Truman and
the President in the year Nineteen
Ninety-eight to request your help.

                    EINSTEIN
To whom would I be helping?

                    BAXTER
He's one Samuel I Hamm. He's
now a graduate student at Harvard.

                    EINSTEIN
A German . . .
        (beat)
Let Hitler help him, whereever he
is in South America.
        (beat)
That is where Hitler is, no, hiding
out with Bormann, Kammler and
Mueller with his plaything Eva
Braun?

Baxter smiles.

                    BAXTER
You know I can't tell you that.

                    EINSTEIN
Why do you require an aged Jew to
help a young German? Cannot

Harvard or Yale assist in this
affair?

> BAXTER
> Times are really quiet in the
> Nineteen Nineties. And he needs
> something to write about.
> (beat)
> Look, we could really use your
> help. Please, I'll take you to
> your house, and you can pack for a
> stay in Boston in the year Nineteen
> Ninety-eight.

Long silence.

> EINSTEIN
> I shall accept on several conditions.
> I require knowing that the atomic
> bomb has not been employed since
> the War, I seek to learn of culture
> and relations between different
> peoples around the world at the
> turn of the millennium, and I
> demand assurance that this student
> is not a National Socialist.

> BAXTER
> Agreed. The future awaits you, Mr.
> Einstein.
> (gesturing to door)
> Come, let's go.

EXT. HOUSE, DANA STREET, CAMBRIDGE, MA (1998) -- DAY

A black Ford sedan pulls up in front of a typical clapboard
Cambridge house near Harvard Square. Einstein and Baxter
exit the vehicle. Baxter pops open the trunk and retrieves
a modern suitcase, obviously his, and a ratty one, obviously
Einstein's, from within. They approach the front door and

Baxter rings the bell. After a beat LEI ZIYANG opens the door.

>   LEI
>   Yes?

>   BAXTER
>   You're Lei Ziyang, one of Sam
>   Hamm's housemates, right?

>   LEI
>   That I am. You must be from the
>   Federal Government, and this I
>   presume is Mr. Einstein. Samuel
>   has been anticipating your arrival,
>   as have we all. Please, enter.

INT. HALLWAY, HOUSE, DANA STREET, CAMBRIDGE, MA (1998) --
DAY

>   LEI
>   Yes, Samuel very much does require
>   your assistance, you know. He has
>   told us all about his having
>   defined forty-eight Nostradamus
>   quatrains that describe his being
>   the Third Antichrist.

>   BAXTER
>   Washington is on the case.

INT. LIVING ROOM, HOUSE, DANA STREET, CAMBRIDGE, MA (1998)
-- DAY

The interior is decorated with stuff you'd expect to find by
graduate students from around the world--Renoir and Delacroix
art posters, a jade Buddha, and a poster of Steve Biko,
a black South African civil rights leader. Baxter stands
giving orders as Lei, Sam, Gabriella, JONAS LOOKSMART and

EAMONN KILMURRAY sit on a sofa and chairs taking in this
amazing event, meeting <u>the</u> Albert Einstein in the flesh.

>   BAXTER
>   Okay, it's gonna go like this,
>   folks. You all are to each keep a
>   journal, and each of you will take
>   Einstein out for a day. Use a
>   Dictaphone to record your
>   experiences with him.   Sam?

>   SAM
>   Yeah?

>   BAXTER
>   I'll sleep on the sofa here, and
>   Einstein will share your bed with
>   you.

>   SAM
>   Einstein's a fag?!

>   BAXTER
>   Look, make like you're in the army.
>   He needs a place to crash, and you
>   got a king-sized bed.
>   (beat)
>   All of you: compare cultural
>   differences between the year
>   Nineteen Forty-eight, which
>   Einstein here's come from, and today.
>   Einstein will have a great many
>   questions for you all. You
>   all in turn will have questions for
>   him. Record everything in your
>   journals and on your Dictaphones.
>   I am to accompany Einstein at all
>   times to protect this national
>   security resource. He takes a

dump, I wipe his ass. That's how
it goes. Nothing can happen to
him.

> GABRIELLA
>
> So, Sam, you ready to finally be
> rich and famous?

> SAM
>
> Hell, fame is this antichrist's
> middle name! Know how much money
> you can make writing a bestseller?!
> And with Einstein helping?!

EXT. MASSACHUSETTS AVENUE, HARVARD SQUARE, CAMBRIDGE, MA
(1998) -- DAY

It's a typical February day with snow on the ground.
Einstein, Carl and Sam are dressed appropriately in winter
apparel. There is tension in the air as the three stride
down the block--an aged Jew, a young German, and a federal
agent. A black Jeep with oversized speakers in its back
seats drives by blaring the SONG "F**k the Police" by Niggaz
Wit Attitude. Einstein peers at the passing vehicle.

> EINSTEIN
>
> This is music? A song about
> shooting police?

> SAM
>
> Freedom of speech, Mr. Einstein.

> EINSTEIN
>
> Is it possible to obtain a pipe and
> some tobacco? I really should not
> smoke, but I do so enjoy it.

                     SAM
          Uh, I can get you those at Leavitt
          and Pierce up ahead. Then we'll
          hit the Out of Town Newsstand and
          The Coop. Then I'll walk you
          around Harvard Yard, and we'll take
          the bus to M.I.T. I'd drive you
          there, but there's no parking.

                     EINSTEIN
          What is this M.I.T.?

                     SAM
          Oh, the Massachusetts Institute of
          Technology.

                     EINSTEIN
          Of course.

INT. OUT OF TOWN NEWSSTAND, HARVARD SQUARE, CAMBRIDGE, MA
(1998) -- DAY

Einstein is poking around the newsstand, picking up the New
York Times and Time magazine, thumbing through the pages.
After a beat Sam goes over to Playboy magazine, yanks it off
the shelf, and returns. He opens it up to the centerfold.

                     SAM
          Hey Einstein, check out that gash.

                     EINSTEIN
          The blonde-haired, blue-eyed
          female. Hmph.

                     SAM
          I was only kidding. Hell, if this
          doesn't rock your boat there's
          always Out magazine.

                    EINSTEIN
          I have just come from the year
          Nineteen Forty-eight, and World War
          Two is fresh on my mind. I care
          not a wit for Aryan fetishes.

Sam replaces the magazine on the rack and returns.

                    EINSTEIN (CONT'D)
          Please, tell me about modern
          culture.

                    SAM
          Well, technological advances have
          exploded since Nineteen Eighty.
          Here,
               (reaching to shelf)
          this is Airliner magazine.

Sam opens it and flips through the pages.

                    SAM (CONT'D)
          See, there's a Boeing Seven Forty-
          seven from Japan Air Lines.

                    EINSTEIN
          Japan is now on friendly terms with
          America?

                    SAM
          Oh yeah, and it's become quite
          economically prosperous, as has
          Germany.
               (beat)
          And that, that's a British Airways
          Concorde, a supersonic jet faster
          than the speed of sound. And,
          uh...
               (more page flipping)

And that's an Airbus A-Three
Eighty. It's a proposed fully
double decker jet to be designed
sometime in the early part of the
next millennium.

Einstein takes the magazine from Sam and thumbs through it.

> EINSTEIN
> Fascinating, though I much prefer
> U.F.O. spacecraft. I am deemed
> quite intelligent, but in truth it
> is because I communicate with God
> and U.F.O.s through telepathy, you
> must know.

> SAM
> You mean you didn't think of all
> that shi--uh, I mean, stuff, on
> your own?

> EINSTEIN
> Can a fool really be as smart as I
> am alleged to be without external
> assistance? It is like the hand
> that raises Alice in Through the
> Looking Glass to facilitate her
> efforts. Sure, Alice would have
> eventually made it up on her own,
> but assistance from wiser external
> sources certainly aids things
> immeasurably, now, does it not?

> SAM
> Hey, uh, one moment.

Sam looks frantically around the newsstand. He approaches
U.F.O. magazine, grabs it off a shelf, and returns.

17

                    SAM (CONT'D)
Look here. Here's U.F.O. magazine.
This describes some of the U.F.O.
stuff you're talking about.

                    EINSTEIN
Does your civilization communicate
regularly with U.F.O.s yet?

                    SAM
Our government does, at a place
called Area Fifty-one in the Nevada
desert. But no, most people around
the world are oblivious to the real
truth about what goes on with the
U.F.O. phenomenon because it's
classified by people like Agent
Baxter here.

Baxter grins.

                    EINSTEIN
One day soon I trust you shall have
societal wide contact with U.F.O.s.
But all in good time.

                    SAM
Well, we are doing well nowadays, I
suppose. The stock market's going
through the roof, and we have peace
around the world. But society is
so sterile today. There's no
really good music anymore on the
radio, and the movies are God
awful. So there's been nothing for
me to write about. No source of
inspiration. Guess that's why
you're here, huh?

                    EINSTEIN
Precisely.
     (beat)
Tell me, what do you intend to do
as the antichrist?

                    SAM
Well, I stop frivolous lawsuits
from resulting in excessive damages
awarded. And I, uh, prevent
overpopulation and subsequent
environmental degradation.

                    EINSTEIN
The Roman Catholic Church and
Negroes are responsible for this,
no?

                    SAM
Yeah. Caucasians and Africans and
Hispanics who believe the Pope when
he says every sperm and every egg
is sacred.

                    EINSTEIN
I see.

INT. THE COOP, HARVARD SQUARE, CAMBRIDGE, MA (1998) -- DAY

Einstein, Baxter and Sam are standing near the art and
architecture section of the bookshelves.

                    EINSTEIN
If every sperm and every egg were
sacred, humanity would have long
ago ruined the planet by the age of
our Founding Fathers.

                    SAM
The Chairman of the Bored
     (fake yawn)
Professor Hodges in my class
Geopolitics and Business in the
Coming Millennium calls 'em our
Founding Parents. God is that guy
politically correct.

                    EINSTEIN
Politically correct?

                    SAM
That's a term that means you
shouldn't say what you want, but
rather you should say what is
polite and sensitive or else you
get sued in a frivolous lawsuit.

                    EINSTEIN
What exactly is a "frivolous
lawsuit?"

                    SAM
It means you have to pay hefty fees
in damages for silly reasons. This
has forced society to become a
"kinder, gentler one," as President
Bush said.

                    EINSTEIN
Let us purchase some art and
architecture books. Then we will
obtain some modern literature.

                    SAM
Well, there's a problem. All the
modern literature's lousy, save
Paulo Coelho's <u>The Alchemist</u> and

Doug Coupeland's <u>Generation X</u>.
We'll get those two books, though.
Coupeland is the writer who gave my
generation it's name, just like
your generation is called The
Silent Generation.

INT. LIVING ROOM, HOUSE, DANA STREET, CAMBRIDGE, MA (1998)
-- NIGHT

Einstein, Baxter, Sam, Gabriella, Jonas, Lei and Eamonn are
there with a mountainous pile of books and videos on the
living room floor.

                    BAXTER
          Okay, Mr. Einstein, you're going to
          read these books and watch these
          videos. We got the good stuff.
          Everything from the documentary
          "Eyes on the Prize" about the Civil
          Rights Movement to modern movies
          from the 'Fifties through today to
          literature, art and architecture.
          It's all here. I'm going to record
          on my Dictaphone any questions or
          comments you have.

                    SAM
               (rising)
          I'm off to do my homework.

                    BAXTER
          Tomorrow, Lei, you'll take Einstein
          and me to Boston's Chinatown. The
          day after, Jonas, you, Einstein,
          Sam and me will take Sam's microbus
          to Roxbury. The day after,
          Gabriella, it's your turn. Then

Eamonn, it's you. You'll be with
Einstein an' me in Southie.

          EAMONN
Southie?

          BAXTER
South Boston.

          GABRIELLA
There's a Portuguese restaurant
called The Midwest Grill in
Cambridge I could take Einstein to
for dinner.

          BAXTER
Wonderful.

          GABRIELLA
Also, I guess I could take him to
the Financial District and the Back
Bay. I need to do some shopping on
Newbury Street anyway, so that will
give Einstein a chance to see the
finer things in today's world.

Einstein groans.

                                DISSOLVE TO:
EXT. TYLER STREET, CHINATOWN, BOSTON, MA (1998) -- DAY

Street performer KEVIN SO strums his guitar and sings
"Average Asian American" as Einstein, Baxter, and Lei slowly
meander down the street.

          EINSTEIN
Tell me now, what was it like being
raised in Peking?

                    LEI
Today it is referred to as
"Beijing." I was born in Nineteen
Sixty-seven, and in my youth
experienced the Cultural
Revolution. This occurred from
Nineteen Sixty-five to Nineteen
Seventy-six. It was a decade of
rampant communism in which the
government was attempting to stamp
out "capitalist roaders."

                    EINSTEIN
The result?

                    LEI
Everything that resembled a middle
class lifestyle or above was
squashed. Priceless art works were
destroyed. Children were instructed
to report their parents to government
officials if they did not succumb
to Maoism--the ruler of China at
the time was Chairman Mao--as
taught in Mao's Little Book of
Quotes. The Red Guard was created
of youth and students to transform
every aspect of a capitalist society
into a communist one with grave
consequences, including imprisonment,
for those who did not conform. I
should show you the book Life and
Death in Shanghai.

                    EINSTEIN
What of your parents?

FLASHBACK: HUTONG, BEIJING, CHINA (1974) -- NIGHT

A hutong in Beijing. Simple building, with Lei's family
simply dressed and no excessive wealth. But: it's the home
of a professor, Lei's mother, who has art works and books
on bookshelves. The RED GUARDS storm in, searching Lei's
family's hutong thoroughly, then take LEI'S MOTHER away for
questioning.

> LEI (V.O.)
> We were all at the dinner table
> when the Red Guard came. They
> searched our entire hutong and took
> away my mother's art and books. As
> a professor at Beijing University,
> she was arrested and interrogated
> for about a week. My family and I
> thought we would never see her
> again.

BACK TO SCENE:

> EINSTEIN
> And what of China today?

> LEI
> Today China is a combination of
> memories and modern. Hong Kong,
> which resembles New York City's
> skyline, is capitalist. It
> reverted to Chinese government
> control last year, so it is no
> longer under Westminster's
> leadership. The Special Economic
> Zones in China, in Shenzhen, Shantou,
> Zhuhai, and Xiamen are experimental
> capitalist regions to see if China
> can have capitalist tendencies

while still retaining a communist
government.

                    EINSTEIN
And these changes have taken place
since Nineteen Seventy-six?

                    LEI
Actually, since about Nineteen
Eighty-nine. The changes, they
are so...rapid. And what is
happening?! The people don't even
know, for they are left in the dark
unless they are in the business or
university environment.

                    BAXTER
Hey, this restaurant, China Pearl,
looks pretty good. Come on, let's
grab a bite to eat.

INT. LIVING ROOM, HOUSE, DANA STREET, CAMBRIDGE, MA (1998)
-- NIGHT

                    BAXTER
We had a real good day, Einstein,
Lei and me. We sawr Chinatown, and
Lei gave Einstein a run-down on
China in Mao's time and today.
Lei, get the book Life and Death in
Shanghai and a book on modern China
from the K-School library for
Einstein here. Jonas, Sam?

                    JONAS/SAM
Yes?

                    BAXTER
          You two're up at bat. Tomorrow, we
          see Roxbury. Wanna show Einstein
          post-Rodney King Riots black urban
          culture.

                                        DISSOLVE TO:

INT. SAM I HAMM'S V.W. MICROBUS, DUDLEY STREET, ROXBURY,
BOSTON, MA (1998) -- DAY

Sam's 1977 V.W. microbus is painted maroon, cream and white,
the colors of San Francisco Municipal Railway diesel buses in
the early 1970s. Sam is driving and Einstein's in the front
passenger seat. The Neville Brothers' SONG "Sister Rosa"
is on the reconfigured C.D.-playing dashboard RADIO. The
neighborhood's gentrifying, slowly but surely. Graffiti covers
building walls, and trash is in the gutters. Black males
mill about on the sidewalks here at high noon, but it's not
half as bad as the early 1980s.

                    JONAS
          Mr. Einstein, what you are looking
          at is hope. You see, these are
          Africans in America, the land of
          opportunity. The real problem is
          that they were invisible up until
          the Rodney King Riots.

                    EINSTEIN
          Rodney King Riots?

                    JONAS
          A black motorist was beaten
          horrifically by four Los Angeles
          police officers. This was filmed
          on videocamera by a civilian and
          sent to the evening news. A
          Caucasian jury in lily white Simi
          Valley, California found the police

innocent. The result was riots
nationwide in protest of police
brutality.

>   SAM
> But it was more than that. What they
> were really protesting is
> Ralph Ellison's "invisibility."
> Ellison wrote The Invisible Man. In
> it he said that blacks are
> invisible for whites do not see
> them nor recognize their culture,
> and do not view them as equals.

>   EINSTEIN
> I have never read his works.

>   SAM
> Yeah, and, well, blacks were
> rioting in cities nationwide in
> Nineteen Ninety-two for similar
> reasons. It wasn't just about police
> brutality. It was really about the
> "Oasis on the Horizon" Syndrome.

>   EINSTEIN
> What precisely is that?

>   SAM
> In every inner-city environment
> where predominantly blacks live you
> can see downtown on the horizon.
> Downtown is where the money is,
> where the power is, where the
> whites work. Whether it's Watts
> in Los Angeles or Chicago's South
> Side or even here in Roxbury, in the
> distance looms downtown's skyline.

JONAS
And for African Americans, that
seems a million miles away. All
African Americans know is
dilapidated housing projects, crack
cocaine vials in the gutter--

BAXTER
That's a highly addictive form of
cocaine that's smoked and can kill
you, Mr. Einstein. All you want is
rock when you've got that monkey on
your back.

EINSTEIN
Rock?

BAXTER
It's sold illegally in white cubes
the size of a small rock, hence
it's nickname.

JONAS
Yes, and spent bullet shells on the
sidewalk from drive-by shootings--

EINSTEIN
The police <u>shoot</u> people?

BAXTER
No, rival gangs do in gangland-
style warfare. Sort of a modern Al
Capone-type warfare between rival
black and hispanic gangs.

JONAS
And the graffiti everywhere with
gang tags on buildings and buses--

                    BAXTER
A tag is like a person's code name
written with spray paint or felt
tip pens.

                    JONAS
African American urban America was
a wasteland in the early Nineteen
Nineties, and the Rodney King Riots
were the result of a cry of
despair.

                    BAXTER
We've got to get the movies
"Colors" and "Boyz in the 'Hood"
for Einstein to see.

                    JONAS
Precisely. So that was black
America in the 'Sixties, 'Seventies
and 'Eighties. Today, there is a
new breeze blowing in urban
America. There are a great many
problems still. However, times are
changing for the better. The
emphasis now is on education,
reaching children early on from
troubled families, cleaning off the
graffiti, drug awareness education,
planned pregnancies and urban
renewal.

                    EINSTEIN
What is it like being a Negro from
South Africa?

                    JONAS
Well, I am from the Alexandra
township north of Joh-burg.

                    BAXTER
That's Johannesburg in slang.

                    JONAS
We recently ended Apartheid in
South Africa, and elected Nelson
Mandela, an African National
Congress party member, to the
presidency.

                    SAM
He had been imprisoned on Robben
Island off South Africa's coast
for, what, over thirty years.
Today he's South Africa's first
black president.

                    JONAS
Yes. Well, today in South Africa
we don't have the gangland violence
of America, but it remains an
economically divided country along
racial lines. Today we have
equality where blacks and whites
look upon each other as equals.
This is something that does not yet
exist in America.

                    EINSTEIN
What is the condition between
Negroes and whites today in
America?

                    JONAS
Blacks are seen as inferior and
undereducated in America, with
black ghettoes in the urban core
and lily white suburbs in cities'
outer perimeters.

                    EINSTEIN
And in South Africa?

                    JONAS
It is largely the same. Blacks
live in townships, like SoWeTo or
Alexandra, and whites live in leafy
suburbs with high gates to protect
their property and lives from
blacks.

                    BAXTER
It's the same in Rio de Janeiro
with the favelas on the hills and
wealthy properties along the
beachfront. Gabriella will tell
you all about that tomorrow.

                    JONAS
Black this, white that. This will
end with education for blacks. And
end with inferior public schools
being taught by incompetent
teachers.

                    BAXTER
It'll also end when the damn kids
stop bringin' guns and drugs to
school and terrorizin' all the good
teachers away.

                    SAM
Like in the book The Blackboard
Jungle.

INT. LIVING ROOM, HOUSE, DANA STREET, CAMBRIDGE, MA (1998)
-- NIGHT

Everyone's back in the living room. The students hold their
notepads and Dictaphones.

>   BAXTER
> Okay, Gabriella, tomorrow it's your
> turn. Einstein, there's a
> Portuguese neighborhood in
> Cambridge, but it's predominantly
> just shops and restaurants. So it
> makes more sense for Gabriella here
> to show you downtown and the Back
> Bay. So: you two have a real nice
> meal at the, what's it called?

>   GABRIELLA
> Midwest Grill.

>   BAXTER
> Yeah, for dinner. Boston and that.

>   EINSTEIN
> I do not require seeing buildings
> of capitalism and stores.

>   GABRIELLA
> What else and I supposed to show you?

>   BAXTER
>   (half-pleading)
> Einstein, just do it. Gabriella,
> take notes, and remember your
> Dictaphone. Einstein, you have a
> homework assignment tonight. Watch
> the film "The House of the Spirits."

                                        DISSOLVE TO:

EXT. CONGRESS STREET, FINANCIAL DISTRICT, BOSTON, MA (1998)
-- DAY

Einstein looks bored. Gabriella is babbling AD LIB about
the stock market and how much money people are making. This
is where the big bucks are made, the Financial District.
Suits and skirts walk briskly past jabbering maniacally into
cell phones on the sidewalk. Money, money, money.

> EINSTEIN
> I have a better idea. Are there
> any museums of World War Two in the
> area?

> GABRIELLA
> Well, there's the Holocaust
> Memorial near Faneuil Hall.

> EINSTEIN
> Let us visit that.

Gabriella hails a taxi and Einstein, Baxter and she pile in.

EXT. HOLOCAUST MEMORIAL, FANEUIL HALL, BOSTON, MA (1998) --
DAY

> Gabriella smokes a butt, looking bored, as Einstein
> gazes at the Memorial in solemn earnestness. He rubs a
> finger along the glass and peers at the numbers of the
> Holocaust victims.

> EINSTEIN
> (reflective)
> This is what my people lived
> through...

Gabriella stomps out her ciggy on the sidewalk and, on
second thought, picks up the butt, realizing she has to show

respect. She looks around for what to do with it, and finally
locates a nearby trash can and returns.

                    GABRIELLA
               (superficially)
          It was very sad indeed. A great
          many Jews died.

                    EINSTEIN
               (solemnly)
          Yes...

                    GABRIELLA
          But people have died all over the
          world. Fifty million died under
          Stalin, thirty million died under
          Mao Zedong in China. Then there was
          recently a genocide in Kosovo in
          which millions perished. So yes,
          it's sad, but people around the
          world have died and will continue
          to die because of war. So it's not
          just the Jews. And further, people
          are starving to death in Africa and
          Central and South America today.

                    EINSTEIN
          'Tis a pity. However, it is not
          just that Jews died in the
          Holocaust. It is how they died.
          Starved to death in concentration
          camps. Medical experiments
          conducted on them by Josef Mengele
          in the name of accelerating human
          evolution and creating a master
          race. Told to swim across lakes in
          the bitter cold at gunpoint until
          they drowned. Mankind never knew
          worse than the National Socialists.

GABRIELLA
(more somber now)
You're right, it hasn't.

EINSTEIN
And now your German boyfriend is
Nostradamus' Third Antichrist. I
was briefed on his file by the
Central Intelligence Agency. He
has serious growth to undergo if he
is ever to work toward ending
overpopulation and leading a
movement to preserve the
environment.

GABRIELLA
All he ever seems to care about is
money and fame. These things he'll
have, of course, when he writes
books and maybe even movies.

EINSTEIN
Imagine how rich I could have been
making money on all my ideas.

GABRIELLA
Why didn't you?

EINSTEIN
Can you imagine a Gandhi with the
money bags of a Carnegie?

GABRIELLA
Carnegie gave all his money away at
his life's end. And, this is what
Bono of the band U2, Warren
Buffett, the world's richest man--
(under her breath)
God is that man rich--

>   (back to normal)
> --and Bill Gates of the computer
> technology company Microsoft are
> doing. All to help the people of
> Africa.

>   EINSTEIN
> Does your family do this?

>   GABRIELLA
> Honestly, no. My father's actually
> quite greedy. We used to be part
> of "La Catorce" in El Salvador. We
> had to flee to Rio de Janeiro in
> Nineteen Seventy-seven when civil
> war broke out.

FLASHBACK: INT. TORRES DE LA DALTON RESIDENCE, COLONIA
ESCALON, SAN SALVADOR, EL SALVADOR (1977) -- NIGHT

This is an elegant mansion in an elite San Salvadorian
neighborhood worthy of a "La Catorce" family. Very Central
American and Spanish in architecture and appointments.

>   GABRIELLA (CONT'D/V.O.)
> I remember doing my homework in
> the living room with my uncle. My
> parents were upstairs.

EL GRUPO STUDENT MILITANTS come crashing through the gate of
the outside wall surrounding the compound in a heavy-duty
truck. They shoot the lock off the front door with a rifle
and come bursting into the mansion. Gabriella's uncle RAUL
shoves her under a table with a tablecloth over it. Moments
later the militants shoot him, then go running up the main
staircase yelling AD LIB. GABRIELLA'S FATHER and MOTHER
come dashing down the back staircase leading to the kitchen
in their bathrobes. Gabriella hears them and screams. Her

father pushes over the table, grabs her, and they all race
outside to the family's Mercedes.

                    GABRIELLA (CONT'D/V.O.) (CONT'D)
          We made it to a military base, and
          from there it was decided it was
          too unsafe to remain in El
          Salvador. The rest of our family
          friends moved to Miami. We wound
          up in Rio because my father owned
          coffee fincas and forest land that
          could be harvested into lumber.

BACK TO SCENE:

                    EINSTEIN
          You have great wealth. I don't
          know if I should feel sorry for
          you.

                    GABRIELLA
               (flatly)
          Jews have great wealth and place an
          emphasis on education. One might
          say, sad as the Holocaust was, one
          can't feel sorry for modern-day Jews.

                    EINSTEIN
          We place great emphasis on
          education because should we ever
          lose our money, our houses, our
          homeland, we can always rebuild.
          With no education, there is no
          future for our people.

                    GABRIELLA
               (laughing)

Well, without coffee and
rainforests, I guess there's no
future for my family.

          EINSTEIN
You personally have Sam.

          GABRIELLA
Yes. Well, he's nice. Sort of
nerdy, but nice. My father wants
me to marry him. Says I'll live like
a queen if I do. Sam's family is
very rich, you know.
    (beat)
So, if we marry I'll live well, and
he'll have plenty more money from
selling books and screenplays about
being a Nostradamus prediction and
all. The masses will eat that
stuff right up.

          EINSTEIN
His life cannot be about making
money! He must serve humanity! He
must become like Gandhi, or this
Dr. Martin Luther King, Jr. who
comes along in the Nineteen Fifties--

          GABRIELLA
Who came along.
    (beat)
And, they were both assassinated.
Is that what you want for Sam?
Besides, if he writes books and
screenplays he can reach people.
And he'd have the money to pay for
security, so he'd never be
assassinated. Look, I watched El

Grupo militants shoot my uncle
Raul.

                    EINSTEIN
The sacrifice of one life, if need
be, is worth the longevity of
humanity.
        (beat)
Sam must <u>grow</u>, and <u>become</u>. I've
seen his file. What he is is not
what he becomes.

                    GABRIELLA
Well, why don't you simply tell him
what to become? That way he can do
it.

                    EINSTEIN
It must come from within, not from
without. From the heart, not
another's mind. He knows he must
serve humanity. But all he seems
to care for is fame and making
money.

                    GABRIELLA
Well, that's all most people in
Generation X care about.
We were all raised during the
Reagan Revolution. Youth for
Reaganites, we were called. Either
you had it or you didn't, and if
you weren't born with it you better
get it somehow. Lie, cheat, steal,
win the lottery, marry into it, or
work hard for it.
        (beat)
Look, I grew up in El Salvador, and
now live in Rio with its favelas on

the hills outside the city. You
make poverty sound like a glorified
ideal. Poverty is wretched.
Poverty is no food on the table.
No money for education.

> EINSTEIN
Money is greed and caring not a wit
for one's fellow man!

> GABRIELLA
Without money you can't give to
your fellow man! Harvard has need-
blind acceptance, where it waives
the tuition for underprivileged
applicants who matriculate. That
can't be done without money.
> (beat)
Einstein, listen to me carefully.
You want Sam to save the world,
tell him to go make himself a whole
lot of money so he can afford to.

> EINSTEIN
Why, so you can be his wife?

INT. LIVING ROOM, HOUSE, DANA STREET, CAMBRIDGE, MA (1998)
-- NIGHT

> BAXTER
So, how was your night on the town
with Gabriella and me?

> EINSTEIN
> (snorts, unimpressed)
The chirasscurro look good at the
Portuguese restaurant, but I enjoyed
my salad instead.

                    BAXTER
Swell.
      (chuckling)
Learn anything?

                    EINSTEIN
      (flatly)
I was educated in the ways of
modern capitalism and how the young
view the world.

                    BAXTER
Wonderful... Okay, next up is you,
Eamonn. Take Einstein and me to
South Boston. Irish neighborhood.
Tell him all about "The Troubles"
in Northern Ireland, and anything
else you can thing of.

                    EAMONN
Righto.

                    BAXTER
Einstein, tonight you're to watch
"The Crying Game."

                                        DISSOLVE TO:

EXT. L STREET, SOUTH BOSTON, MA (1998) -- DAY

Einstein, Baxter and Eamonn exit a taxi. Carl hands the
driver a bill, and they begin strolling down L Street.

                    EAMONN
So, this is South Boston. The
Irish, as you know, have a long
history here in Boston.
      (beat)
"Give us your masses, yearning to
be free."

41

> EINSTEIN

Statue of Liberty.

> EAMONN

Ehm, yeah.
> (beat)

So, I guess I'll tell you about
"The Troubles" in Northern Ireland,
and then tell you about the
European Union. Well, ehm, "The
Troubles" began in Nineteen
Sixty-nine between the Irish and the
Protestants living in
Northern Ireland. Belfast and
Derry--

> EINSTEIN

Londonderry?

> EAMONN

We Irish call it Derry. Yes, well,
they got hit particularly bad in
'Sixty-nine. I grew up in the
Beechmount neighborhood in the
Falls Road area, rife with the
Irish Republican Army, or the
I.R.A. as it's known. We Irish
were raised to hate the
Protestants, and the United
Kingdom. We want Northern Ireland
to revert to Irish control.

> EINSTEIN

If everyone in Northern Ireland
wants the country to be Irish, why
won't the United Kingdom simply
allow this to happen?

                    EAMONN
It's the Prods. They see us Taigs
as overpopulating, taking over
Northern Ireland in terms of
population. And they're running
scared, 'cause it's only a matter
of time 'til we are the majority.
The Irish don't practice birth
control, so we have a great many
children. And the Prods hate us
for that. They see us Taigs with
our eight children or so needing to
be fed with no money for food as
wretched. But the Irish believe
it's God's will not to practice
birth control.

                    EINSTEIN
It's not God's will that people
starve to death because you do not
practice birth control, I must
assure you. God's and U.F.O.s'
will is for the longevity of
humanity on the planet Earth, not
for human life to become
unsustainable.

                    EAMONN
Yeah, well, me, I practice birth
control with me mates, but you try
telling that to the Irish back
home.
        (beat)
'Sides, they figure the more
children they have, the more power
they'll eventually have in the
government. More voters, more
Irish in a majority Protestant-
controlled land that shouldn't even

belong to the United Kingdom to
begin with.

> EINSTEIN
> What is the status of "The
> Troubles" today?

> EAMONN
> Well, this bloke Bill Clinton, the
> American president, has worked with
> both sides to resolve the issue.
> So now there's less sectarian
> violence.

> EINSTEIN
> And?

> EAMONN
> So we're learning from the blacks
> of America and South Africa. If
> they can use peaceful means to
> resolve past afflictions by whites,
> we're hoping we can do the same in
> Northern Ireland.

> EINSTEIN
> Violence is senseless.

> EAMONN
> Right. And, ehm, the wee ones
> until very recently grew up knowing
> nothing but violence and poverty.
> What firm is going to invest in
> violence-wracked Northern Ireland?
> They want to make profits in a
> peaceful, productive environment,
> not a bloody war-zone.

EINSTEIN
Tell me about the European Union.

EAMONN
Well, there are fifteen member
nations around Europe. Not all
European countries are members,
mind you, but a great many of the
more prosperous ones are. In the
old days, your times, you needed a
passport to go through customs to
travel from one country to the
next. Now you bypass all that
and keep driving. And with
international business being so
accelerated today, that's really
important.

EINSTEIN
So America is still a superpower
today?

BAXTER
Yeah. And Russia today is no
longer a communist nation.

EAMONN
And America will continue to be,
unless the bloody Chinese and
Indians step up to the plate.
There's no welfare in China or
India. You work, or you starve.
Give 'em twenty years and they'll
show you. All of Asia, for that
matter.

EINSTEIN
What will be required to prevent
overpopulation?

                    EAMONN
People need to learn the truth
about religion from the American
government. They communicate with
U.F.O.s in a classified manner.
The C.I.A. that Agent Baxter here's
a member of, they know the truth.

                    EINSTEIN
It they were to tell the truth it
would decimate culture, it would
wipe out heritage. Religion is
sacred.

                    EAMONN
So I'm not going to hell for
practicing birth control?

                    EINSTEIN
Nothing of the sort. Neither will it
happen to all these homosexuals. The
truth is one
dies, and U.F.O.s reincarnate his
soul into another baby being born.
Then one lives his life all
over again.

                    EAMONN
Why can't a person just live for
eternity?

                    EINSTEIN
Boredom. People need their first
kiss, to drive an auto for the
first time, to get married all over
again, and have different kids. If
one lived forever, one would get
bored.

                    EAMONN
So you communicate with U.F.O.s?

                    EINSTEIN
And with God.

                    EAMONN
Bloody hell... You'll give Sam
plenty to write about, sure enough.
Oh, look, there's the L Street
Tavern, from the movie "Good Will
Hunting." Let's stop in for a wee
spot of ale.

                    EINSTEIN
I do not consume alcohol.

                    EAMONN
Well, then I'll stop in for a cold
one!

INT. LIVING ROOM, HOUSE, DANA STREET, CAMBRIDGE, MA (1998)
-- NIGHT

The students sit around the living room with their legal
pads and Dictaphones. Einstein sits in a chair as Carl barks
orders.

                    BAXTER
Okay, folks, we're on track. Sam,
we need a plan. We can't just have
everyone talking to Einstein and
having him read books and watch
videos. We need to do something.

                    SAM
How about a road trip to New York?

                    BAXTER
          Good idear. Einstein, be thinking
          of what you'd like to see around
          America. Maybe I could arrange for
          a plane to take you all to
          California or Chicago. Youse guys,
          get creative. Okay, Einstein,
          tonight you watch "Good Will
          Hunting" in honor of this fair city
          of Boston and the L Street Tavern.
          Eamonn, good job today.

                                        DISSOLVE TO:

INT. FOGG MUSUEM, HARVARD UNIVERSITY, CAMBRIDGE, MA (1998)
-- DAY

Einstein, Carl and Sam meander from painting to painting
slowly, taking a beat to admire the better ones and
walking past the ones of lesser quality. They're in the
Impressionist Art area.

                    SAM
          Gabriella really likes
          Impressionist art. Renoir and
          Monet are her favorites.

                    EINSTEIN
          Those artistic works were
          originally considered rubbish.
          No surprise she adores them. She is
          not a lady of substance.
               (beat)
          She only likes you for your money,
          you realize.

                    SAM
          Well, I only like her for good sex,
          to be honest. Which I haven't had

                            48

since <u>you've</u> been sharing my bed with me.

                    EINSTEIN
She wants to marry you.

                    SAM
We'll go our separate ways after graduating from the K-School.

                    EINSTEIN
K-School?

                    SAM
John F. Kennedy School of Government.
     (beat)
Anyway, I don't know whom I'll marry.

                    EINSTEIN
I know. But I shan't tell you.

                    SAM
Is she a real physical specimen? You know, with humongous gams and all?

                    EINSTEIN
One day you shall know. But you're not ready for her. She's quite famous.

                    SAM
Famous-famous, or just, you know, famous?

                    EINSTEIN
Very famous. She's an icon of
your generation. But she is very
spiritual, and kind. She is not
impressed a wit by money, though
she has quite a bit. She was born
into poverty, and made it on her
own.

                    SAM
Cool. So how rich is she?

                    EINSTEIN
You do not understand. You are not
ready for her yet. You must become
a loving, genuinely nice, and
sensitive person if you are to
marry her. She would never
consider you in your current state.

                    SAM
Well, if she loves me, doesn't she
have to love me warts and all?

                    EINSTEIN
She'll love you only if you're love-
able.

They shuffle from painting to painting, pausing briefly in
front of each one, and keep talking AD LIB.

                    SAM
This is, what,
        (squinting at a plate
        describing artist and
        painting name)
A Camille Pissarro. Lesse what
it's called.

Sam peers at the plate.

> SAM (CONT'D)
> "Mardi Gras on the Boulevards."
> Huh.

> EINSTEIN
> Does Mardi Gras still occur in New
> Orleans?

> SAM
> Yeah, it does. In fact, it's
> coming up pretty soon, and, well--

A flash of inspiration floods Sam's face.

> SAM (CONT'D)
> Righteous! Dude--uh, I mean,
> Einstein! Let's go to Mardi Gras!
> It's ingenious! Agent Baxter,
> that's it!

> BAXTER
> Okay, you wanna take Einstein, your
> friends, and my stupid ass to New
> Orleans? I can probably arrange a
> plane.

> SAM
> No! No plane! To properly
> chronicle an experience of this
> magnitude we need a <u>ride</u>. Like a
> Winnabego or one of those tour
> buses rock and roll bands have.

> BAXTER
> Smart. That way Einstein can see
> some of the American heartland.

                    SAM
We drive to New York, see the
United Nations there!

                  EINSTEIN
So the United Nations still exists?
Why is there a need for national
governments, then?

                    SAM
Governments want to retain control
over their national borders. The
United Nations is the body that
serves to create rules overseeing
peace around the planet.

                  EINSTEIN
Is it more powerful than the United
States government?

                  BAXTER
While the United Nations has the
ideals, the United States has the
money and guns. It's the Golden
Rule.

                  EINSTEIN
        (knowingly)
He with the gold rules.

                    SAM
So: we need a ride. A bus of some
sort. Baxter, think, how do we get
our hands on a bus?

                  BAXTER
I could probably arrange for us to
borrow an M.B.T.A. bus.

                    SAM
No, there's a bus, see, and then a
bus. Furthur in the Electric Kool-
Aid Acid Test was a bus. We don't
simply need wheels, we need a ride.

                    BAXTER
What precisely do you have in mind,
like a Greyhound-type bus? Could
probably get you one of those and a
driver.

                    SAM
Look, I know buses. I know the
perfect bus. It's the type the San
Francisco Municipal Railway used to
have. It was manufactured by the
General Motors Corporation.
        (beat)
Look, why don't we go to the
M.B.T.A. trackless trolley garage
and find out how to buy a bus and
how much one costs?

EXT. BENNETT GARAGE, MASSACHUSETTS AVENUE, CAMBRIDGE, MA
(1998) -- DAY

Gabriella pulls into the yard in her red 1994 SAAB
convertible. As she pulls to a stop, we can read her
license plate: "SNAAB," with a license plate holder reading
"How Swede It Is." On the rear window are Dartmouth and
Harvard stickers. She and Sam exit the front seats, and
Einstein and Baxter exit the rear ones. Then they all march
toward the office.

INT. OFFICE, BENNETT GARAGE, MASSACHUSETTS AVENUE,
CAMBRIDGE, MA (1998) -- DAY

>   MANAGER
>   Look in the yellow pages under
>   "buses." You know, you can always
>   charter a bus. That way you'll get
>   a driver too.

>   SAM
>   Therein lies a problem. You can't
>   drink beer on a chartered bus. We
>   have a mission to properly
>   chronicle an experience at Mardi
>   Gras. New Orleans is the <u>last</u>
>   place you take somebody else's bus.

>   MANAGER
>   (beat)
>   No kiddin', Sherlock.

>   SAM
>   That's like someone lending you
>   their Rolls Royce keys and telling
>   you to have a safe Mardi Gras.

EXT. BOND'S SALES AND SERVICE, PLYMOUTH, MA (1998) -- DAY

JESSE BOND, the owner of Bond's Sales and Service, is dressed
in a button-down flannel shirt and blue jeans. He is in the
yard of Bond's showing Einstein, Baxter, Sam and Gabriella
used buses for sale.

>   SAM
>   What I'm looking for, see, is not
>   one of these new fangled buses but
>   a G.M.C. Bus from the 'Sixties or
>   'Seventies.

                    JESSE
Some a those 're just plain shot.
Got two of 'em, but you might be
better in something a bit more
modern, just sos you can rest easy
knowin' you won't have a breakdown
somewhere in the middle of Social
Siberia.

                    SAM
Show us the two you got.

                    JESSE
There over yonder.

They walk past used Plymouth and Brockton buses and used
Brush Hill buses, past a few school buses, and finally...

                    JESSE (CONT'D)
This here's a Nineteen Sixty-eight
one from Providence. She has an
average number of miles on her for
her age and--

                    SAM
          (pointing)
This one! This one here! This one
shreds! What can you tell me about
it?!

                    JESSE
Well, it's a Nineteen Seventy-two
G.M.C. Fishbowl bus, as you
recognize, from the New York City
Metropolitan Transit Authority.
She's a Suburban bus, meaning
there's no back door, and has Bus-O-
Rama advertising billboards on
either side of her roof. She's got

high-backed seats like on a
Greyhound bus, and--

      SAM

How much?

      JESSE

Cost you twelve and a half, as is,
no warranty.

      SAM

What do you need to drive this
thing?

      JESSE
    (like duh)
Uh, a driver...

      SAM

No, I mean, are there any special
driver's license requirements?

      JESSE

If you're transportin' ten or fewer
passengers in the Commonwealth of
Massachusetts you don't need a
Class B license.

      SAM

How about in the Commonwealth of
Pardi Gras?

      JESSE

Wha?

      SAM

Uh, never mind. I'll take it.

```
                    JESSE
          Sold.
               (beat)
          Was intendin' to sell it to a
          charter company up in Alaska, but
          if you're cuttin' a check first I
          might as well sell it to you.
```

MONTAGE:

Done to The Meters' SONG "They All Ask for You."

A) Scene of the students, Einstein and Baxter inside Eastern Mountain Sports buying sleeping bags.

B) Scene of the group decorating the bus. Lei and Jonas tape bumper stickers to the right windshield's interior. They read "Hussong's Cantina," "K-FOG San Francisco," "Wall Drug," and "South of the Border."

C) Sam hangs long beads over the interior rearview mirror and places a can of Underwood's Deviled Ham and several map books on the dashboard.

D) Gabriella places a "Harvard" sticker on the rear window's interior

E) Baxter and Eamonn tape a banner to the rear window's interior reading "Pardi Gras or BUSt!"

F) Scene of the group loading a keg of tapped beer onto the bus' wheelchair ramp mechanism and raising the keg into the bus' interior in front of Kappy's Liquors in Cambridge, MA.

EXT. INTERSTATE 95 SOUTH, PROVIDENCE, RI (1998) -- DUSK

The bus drives along the highway to Howlin' Wolf's SONG "Six Days on the Road."

INT. BUS, INTERSTATE 95 SOUTH, CT (1998) -- NIGHT

Sam is at the wheel as everyone else save Einstein and
Baxter plays the drinking game "Quarters." Eamonn has
brought a board from his bookshelf, and he and Gabriella are
really getting into the game. Lei and Jonas play as well,
though less enthusiastically.

>   SAM
>   We'll be in New York by ten. We'll
>   park in the loading zone on the
>   other side of the Yale Club and get
>   rooms there.
>
>   EINSTEIN
>   You graduated from Yale as well? I
>   thought you only graduated from
>   Duke and the London School of
>   Economics?
>
>   SAM
>   I'm a legacy member. My father
>   graduated from Yale and he
>   got me in.
>   (beat)
>   Gabriella, you and I will share a
>   room--
>
>   GABRIELLA
>   One can only guess what's on your
>   mind...
>
>   SAM
>   --Lei, you, Eamonn and Jonas will
>   share a room. One of you's
>   sleeping on the sofa.

EAMONN
Sorry about that, Lei. Tough luck,
old chappie.

SAM
And Agent Baxter, you and Einstein
will share a room. Breakfast will
be at eight-thirty. Then we'll see
the United Nations.

EINSTEIN
I should enjoy that more than all
this drinking tomfoolery.

SAM
Jonas, make a note of that comment.

EINSTEIN
I am not traveling to the City of New
Orleans to partake in college hijinx
and drinking. Only to see
the architecture and culture.

SAM
Uh, this could be a problem.
    (beat)
Anyway, I called my friend from
Duke, Forrest Robecheaux. He lives
in New Orleans, and every year he
gets a second floor room with a
balcony overlooking the corner of
Bourbon and Orleans Streets at the
Bourbon Orleans Hotel.

EINSTEIN
Our accommodations in New Orleans.

                         SAM
          Further, it's imperative that
          everyone obtain as many long beads
          as possible.

                         EINSTEIN
          For what purpose? To dress as
          fools?

                         BAXTER
          Women lift their shirts if you throw
          'em beads, Einstein.

                         EINSTEIN
          Good Lord, I should have never
          agreed to come.

                         SAM
          Eamonn?

                         EAMONN
               (guzzling his beer's remainder)
          I'll make a note of that comment.

INT. UNITED NATIONS, NEW YORK, NY (1998) -- DAY

The group is in front of the Norman Rockwell painting
depicting peoples from around the world praying to God as
their cultures dictate.

                         BAXTER
          Lucky we found a minivan taxi to
          take all of us. If the bus gets
          towed from that loading zone across
          from the Yale Club I'll make a
          call.

                         SAM
          Most appreciated.

> (to Einstein)
> Now, this is a famous Norman
> Rockwell painting depicting peoples
> from around the world praying.
> Soon we'll be in the General
> Assembly Room where the security
> council meets. That room is famous
> for its unfinished ceiling.

                    EAMONN
> Why's it unfinished?

                    SAM
> It symbolizes that the work of the
> United Nations is never done.

The group heads down the hall to toward the General Assembly
Room.

EXT. UNITED NATIONS, NEW YORK, NY (1998) -- DAY

The group stands in front of the statue of the twisted gun.

                    EINSTEIN
> I very much like this statue. If
> only two percent of men refused to
> fight, there would be no wars.

                    GABRIELLA
> Today women are in the armed forces
> as well. God bless them. Tough
> job.

                    EINSTEIN
> I just wrote that the United
> Nations should have supranational
> control over nuclear weapons, not
> individual countries. Then rogue

nations would be deterred from
starting wars.

> EAMONN
> What do you mean you <u>just</u> wrote
> that?

> BAXTER
> He means he wrote it back in 'Forty-
> eight, where he's just come from.

> EAMONN
> Oh.

The group walks over to the sidewalk and Sam waits a beat
for just the right cab to pass--a minivan--before raising his
hand to hire it. It pulls over.

INT. BUS, NEW JERSEY TURNPIKE, NJ (1998) -- DAY

The group is noshing on monstrous sandwiches from Carnegie
Deli, using Carnegie Deli napkins to wipe their faces.
Einstein crunches into a massive pickle, and Baxter chomps at
his strawberry-topped cheesecake.

> SAM
> We'll be in Washington, D.C. in six
> hours. We'll drive through it.
> Show you, Einstein, the White House
> and The Capitol and what the
> nation's capital looks like today.

> EINSTEIN
> Fine, fine.

> SAM
> Then we'll spend a night at a
> Maryland truck stop.

MONTAGE:

A) The bus drives past The Capitol.

B) Then the bus drives past the White House.

C) Then the bus drives through the intersection of Georgetown's Wisconsin and M Streets.

> SAM (V.O.)
> This is Georgetown, where Georgetown University is.

EXT. BUS, INTERSTATE 85 SOUTH, NC (1998) -- DAY

> SAM (V.O.)
> Okay, we'll see Duke University, where I graduated from, and have lunch at Bullock's Barbecue in Durham.

> EINSTEIN (V.O.)
> All that meat. That is all you people eat. I am a vegetarian, you realize.

> SAM (V.O.)
> Lei, note that comment for the record. The experience must be properly chronicled.

> LEI (V.O.)
> Experience noted as such...

EXT. CHAPEL, DUKE UNIVERSITY, DURHAM, NC (1998) -- DAY

> SAM
> This is the Duke Chapel, the most notable building on campus. And

this, this here's West Campus.
Duke represents a university in the
American heartland, where people
are moving to because the cost of
raising a family is affordable and
taxes and cost of living is lower
than in New England, New York and
California.

                    EINSTEIN
But plenty of people live in New
York and California. They are
overpopulated.

                    SAM
They're overpopulated with
professionals. But after people
obtain their skills, they move to
towns and smaller cities in the
Step States for more affordable
living with lower taxes.

                    BAXTER
"Step States?" Never heard that
term before.

                    JONAS
It's a term Dr. Hodges uses to
describe the Northwest over and
down to the Rockies over and down
to the Midwest over and down to the
Southeast.

The group begins to walk toward West Campus as SAE
FRATERNITY BROTHERS blare AC/DC's SONG "Hells Bells" from a
radio while playing Beer Frisbee as the Chapel's bells loudly
gong.

INT. BULLOCKS BARBECUE, DURHAM, NC (1998) -- DAY

The group pigs out on Southern style eatin'. Ribs, fried chicken, hush puppies, the works. Einstein has a large salad and a small bowl of cole slaw in front of him. Carl pours gobs of hot sauce onto his Brunswick stew. The group sits at a table where Dolly Parton and Bruce Hornsby have signed autographs on pictures on the wall, and there's another of the Duke men's basketball team and its coach Mike Krzyzewski holding a 1992 National Championship trophy.

>   SAM
> We'll be in Atlanta by midnight.
> We'll park the bus in a loading
> zone or a bus stop in some
> residential neighborhood.

>   GABRIELLA
> My back is killing me from sleeping
> on the bus' hard floor.

>   JONAS
> We are still seeing Maya Lin's
> Civil Rights Memorial in
> Montgomery, Alabama, tomorrow, no?

>   SAM
> Yes, and we're seeing the State
> Capital's steps from which Governor
> George Wallace proclaimed
> "Segregation now, segregation
> tomorrow, segregation forever."

>   LEI
> I cannot wait to drive down
> Cleveland Avenue, where Rosa Parks
> refused to give up her seat on a
> bus.

                    SAM
        We're doing it all.
            (beat)
        Jonas, all this is very important
        to you, so be sure to take diligent
        notes on your impressions.

                    JONAS
        I shall.

EXT. CIVIL RIGHTS MEMORIAL, MONTGOMERY, AL (1998) -- DAY

The group stands before the Civil Rights Memorial. Jonas
is eagerly taking in the entries on the black marble
sculpture shaped like an oversized round table. Gabriella
shows slightly more interest than she did at the Holocaust
Memorial. Einstein slowly reads around the Memorial. This
is a part of history that lies in a future he'll die to soon
to see.

                    JONAS
        It's too bad we don't have time to
        see the Edmund Pettus Bridge in
        Selma.

                    BAXTER
        Einstein, that's where Dr. Martin
        Luther King, Jr. led a group of
        marchers from Selma toward the
        State Capital of Alabama to protest
        segregation of blacks and whites.
        State troopers beat the marchers.
        Later the marchers were finally
        allowed to march from Selma to
        Montgomery. It took fifteen years,
        from Nineteen Fifty-five to
        Nineteen Seventy, for blacks to
        achieve equal rights.

                    LEI
          And then a legacy of racism
          prevented blacks from achieving
          true equality up until about
          Nineteen Seventy-eight.

                    JONAS
          And then inner city problems
          prevailed, as did poverty in the
          South for blacks, up until the
          Rodney King Riots.

                    SAM
          We'll be in New Orleans by
          midnight. Come on, let's see the
          State Capital.

EXT. BUS, INTERSTATE 10 WEST, LA (1998) -- DAY

The bus passes a "Welcome to Louisiana" interstate sign.
There is a VOICE OVER of the students cheering.

EXT. BUS, INTERSTATE 10 WEST, NEW ORLEANS, LA (1998) --
NIGHT

Con Funk Shun's SONG "Ffun" is heard as the bus takes the
offramp for New Orleans.

MONTAGE:

Heard to Con Funk Shun's "Ffun."

A) Pete Fountain's Half Fast Marching Band tootling down
Bourbon Street in the French Quarter

B) historic streetcars passing along St. Charles Street in
Uptown

C) historic buildings at Tulane University

D) the waterfront at Canal Street's end

E) the historic Jax Brewery Building

F) majestic Garden District homes

G) the lily white Rex Parade

H) young African American flambeaux bearers of the black-as-can-be Zulu Parade

I) gangs of African American Mardi Gras Indians dancing flamboyantly on Canal Street

J) the gritty Lower Ninth Ward neighborhood with destitute African American males drinking 40 ounce beers on stoops in front of dilapidated shotgun houses as freshly painted Zulu coconuts dry in the sun

K) and throngs of revelers--black and white--on Bourbon street in the French Quarter.

The feel of the above is this is a city divided between wealthy Caucasians and poor African Americans who come together only to have a good time.

INT. BUS, CANAL STREET, NEW ORLEANS, LA (1998) -- NIGHT

> SAM
> (holding clear plastic cup
> with beer)
> There's a traffic jam up ahead.
> Agent Baxter, find out what's going
> on.

Sam opens the front doors. Baxter steps off, surveys the situation, and reports back.

                    BAXTER
There's a parade of some sort up
ahead. Traffic's wicked bad.

                    SAM
          (chugging beer)
This calls for most drastic
measures. Okay, everyone, I'm
gonna drive on the opposite side of
the street. When we get to the
parade's end, clear a path so I can
keep going.

                                        SMASH CUT TO:

EXT. BUS, CANAL STREET, NEW ORLEANS, LA (1998) -- NIGHT

The students, all holding clear plastic cups filled with
frothy ale, are telling people AD LIB to step aside and make
way as the bus drives up to the Endymion Parade's rear end.
The Endymion Parade is inching its way along. All the group
can do is wait it out.

                    EAMONN
     Shite, we'll be here all night.

Eamonn approaches the bus and hops in the front door.

INT. BUS, CANAL STREET, NEW ORLEANS, LA (1998) -- NIGHT

                    EAMONN
     We're stuck. Know any side streets
     we can take?

                    SAM
     Not in a bus. We have to make it
     to the bus stop at Bourbon and
     Canal Streets, where Forrest said
     we should ditch the bus. From

there, we head over to the Bourbon
Orleans Hotel to meet Forrest and
his friend Alain.

          EAMONN
Bloody hell.

                          DISSOLVE TO:

EXT. BALCONY, ROOM 203, BOURBON ORLEANS HOTEL, FRENCH
QUARTER, NEW ORLEANS, LA (1998) -- NIGHT

FORREST ROBECHEUAX is talking AD LIB with ALAIN LIVOUDAIS,
his friend, while throwing beads to WOMEN who are lifting
their shirts on the street below, when they hear a KNOCK on
the room's door.

          FORREST
Das right, girls, show them God-
given racks!
    (swigging from a beer
    bottle; to Alain)
Be right back.
    (to women on street below)
Don't you go nowheres now, bitties!

INT. ROOM 203, BOURBON ORLEANS HOTEL, FRENCH QUARTER, NEW
ORLEANS, LA (1998) -- NIGHT

Forrest trudges across the room and opens the door.

          FORREST
Hot damn, Sam! Haven't seen
you/since the Class of 'Ninety-
two/at dear old D.U.! Where you
at?

          SAM
Thanks for the invite!

Sam introduces everyone AD LIB to Forrest.

>   FORREST
>   (to Einstein)
>   So you're the <u>real</u> Albert Einstein,
>   huh? Sam here's told me all about
>   you.

>   EINSTEIN
>   So you have read your history
>   books, I presume...

>   FORREST
>   Can I offer you a beer?

>   BAXTER
>   He doesn't drink.

>   FORREST
>   Well then, can I get <u>you</u> a beer?
>   Got Dixies, best damn brew in the
>   South.

The group heads into the room and tosses their sleeping
bags onto the floor. Alain enters the room from the balcony,
holding a camera phone in one hand--he's been taking
photographic souvenirs of the lovelies on the street--and
a glass filled with bourbon and ice cubes in the other. He
sets the glass down on the living room table.

>   ALAIN
>   (shaking everyone's hand)
>   The pleasures mine. Alain
>   Livoudais. Friend of Forrest's
>   here.

Einstein looks around the room a beat, surveying his new
accommodations.

> EINSTEIN
>
> Well, I think I shall rest.
> Goodnight, all.

> ALAIN
>
> (to Sam)
>
> That fellow serious? Bedtime
> doesn't start 'til five thirty in
> the morn and rising time ain't 'til
> it's first call at Pat O'Brien's
> during Mardi Gras.

> SAM
>
> C'mon, let's go to Pat O'Brien's
> and let Einstein here rest his
> little grey cells.

> ALAIN
>
> What in hell's that boy thinkin'?,
> comin' to Mardi Gras only to sleep.

> SAM
>
> We're on a quest to chronicle the
> experience. I'll explain over
> drinks.

EXT. PATIO, PAT O'BRIEN'S SALOON, FRENCH QUARTER, NEW
ORLEANS, LA (1998) -- NIGHT

Forrest, Alain, Baxter, and the students sit around a black
iron patio furniture table drinking hurricanes.

> FORREST
>
> That Einstein doesn't steer clear
> of the rear if you ask me.
> Sleeping on a gorgeous New Orleans
> night like this...

                    BAXTER
He's older than you young bucks.

                    FORREST
So, it's up to Alain here an' me to
show you all a good time in the
Crescent City. You park where I
tole you, Sam?

                    SAM
Yeah.

                    FORREST
Perfectamundo.

They all continue to take chugs of their hurricanes, and
engage a beat in small talk AD LIB.

                    JONAS
Forrest, have race relations
improved in New Orleans since the
Rodney King Riots?

                    FORREST
Well now, that there's an
interesting question.
          (pops Alain a knowing look)
New Orleans has never been a
tolerant city. See, lots of people
say New Orleans and San Francisco,
where Sam here was raised, are
sister cities. Both have real nice
architecture, good eatin', a laid
back lifestyle, and loads a
culture. But you got to
understand, that's where the
similarities end.

                    ALAIN
Tha's right. What Forrest is
sayin' is when you look at San
Francisco, it's like the
international terminal at an
airport. Everyone there's
transient. It's too expensive for
the hippies, beatniks, artists and
musicians, so what do you have
instead?

                    FORREST
Yuppies. Alain's correct. It's
all yuppies living in San
Francisco, attracted to the city
for the good life, and for
toleration of quee--I mean, gay
folk.
        (beat)
But New Orleans, now, we're like a
checkerboard. Honestly, we are.
Whites over here, in the Garden
District and Uptown, and blacks
over yonder, in Mid City and
Storyville and the Lower Ninth
Ward.

                    ALAIN
People think when they come to New
Orleans that it's gonna be all laid
back and loving, 'cause New
Orleanians have a reputation for
Southern charm, but that's not the
case. Each side of the
checkerboard has its kings. The
blacks got the king of the Zulu
parade and the mayor's office. The
whites got plantations and oil
fields.

                    FORREST
An' tha's the South.
        (half-heartedly attempting
         to be politically
         correct)
Now, time's <u>are</u> changin', see.
Blacks are gettin' good jobs, and
we have a colored mayor. Poverty
stricken whites are goin' sideways
'cause they don't got an education,
and educated whites are buyin' up
what lazy rich whites can no longer
afford. So things <u>are</u> slowly
becomin' more integrated, but
again, it's slow.

Everyone takes a slow drink from his or her hurricane. The
mood has grown dismal.

Gabriella then decides to leaven things, and rises.

                    GABRIELLA
I'm going to ask the piano player
in the lounge if I can sing.
Anyone care to join me?

                    BAXTER
        (attempting to keep things
         upbeat)
Here, we all will.

INT. LOUNGE, PAT O'BRIEN'S SALOON, FRENCH QUARTER, NEW
ORLEANS, LA (1998) -- NIGHT

Gabriella approaches the fifty-something rotund African
American PIANO PLAYER who's AD LIB thanking people for
applauding to a number he's just finished.

                    GABRIELLA
      Sir, do you know Sinatra's "They've
      Got a Lot of Coffee in Brazil?"

                    PIANO PLAYER
      Sheeit, do C-Notes have Franklins
      on 'em?

Gabriella climbs on top of the grand piano and sprawls across its lid.

                    GABRIELLA
      Hit it, maestro.

The piano player starts playing "They've Got a Lot of Coffee in Brazil."

Gabriella begins to sing "They've Got a Lot of Coffee in Brazil."

                                        CUT TO:

INT. LOUNGE, PAT O'BRIEN'S SALOON, FRENCH QUARTER, NEW ORLEANS, LA (1998) -- NIGHT

Gabriella finishes the song "They've Got a Lot of Coffee in Brazil." At the end of her performance, PEOPLE whistle and cheer. Gabriella, with her Hermes scarf, white blouse, and chic blue jeans, looks quite the morsel. DRUNKEN MEN are going crazy.

                    GABRIELLA
        (bowing side to side)
      Thank you so much, thank you...

                    FORREST
      Let's hit Cafe du Monde, y'all, for
      some beignets and cafe au laits, then
      call it a night. Got a full day

tomorrow of stuff I want to
show y'all, including the Bacchus
Parade.

                                              DISSOLVE TO:

EXT. ROBECHEAUX MAUSOLEUM, METAIRIE CEMETERY, NEW ORLEANS,
LA (1998) -- DAY

A slight wind blows the hair of Forrest, Alain, and the
group. They are all silent as they stand in front of the
decrepit mess of a mausoleum that houses the remains of the
once rich Robecheauxs. It's lack of repair suggests the
family has lost its financial luster.

                    FORREST
          My great-great grandparents, my
          great-grandparents, and my
          grandparents are all buried here.
          My grandfathers used to be plantation
          owners. I know that must make you
          real mad, Jonas, but that's the way it
          was in Louisiana back then.

                    BAXTER
               (attempting to inject
                political correctness)
          Times have changed indeed.

                    FORREST
          Yeah, I guess they have...
               (beat)
          It's still not so great if you're a
          colored in New Orleans, though.
          The Lower Ninth Ward, Mid City,
          Storyville, now those are some
          rough neighborhoods.

                    ALAIN
Wouldn't catch any of us dead in
those places.
        (beat)
Well, maybe we <u>would</u> be dead if we
were.
        (chuckles slightly)

                    FORREST
My father's into oil now.

                    GABRIELLA
You must have quite a family
history.

                    FORREST
We were one of the richest families
in Louisiana in my grandfather's
days.

                    SAM
Gabriella here's family was part of
"La Catorce" in El Salvador.

                    ALAIN
"La Catorce" is Spainiard for what?

                    JONAS
For "The Fourteen." There used to
be fourteen ruling families in all
El Salvador.
        (indignantly)
That's why the peasants rebelled,
for they had no food, no education
nor opportunities while the elite
lived like kings.

                    GABRIELLA
I live in Rio now.

                    FORREST
Where's that, near the Rio Grande
in Texas?

                    GABRIELLA
        (huffing)
Rio de Janeiro.

                    FORREST
Oh, right.

The group is silent a beat.

                    FORREST (CONT'D)
Some of the older families have
mausoleums that have fallen into
disrepair. You can always tell
who's new money. They gots to have
the flashiest mausoleums, and they
keep 'em spic and span.

                    ALAIN
Well, Forrest, when you die,
they'll bury you here.
        (beat)
Tell you all what. Let's hit the
Bacchus Parade.

EXT. NAPOLEON STREET, UPTOWN, NEW ORLEANS, LA (1998) -- DAY

REVELERS are yelling "Throw me somethin', mister!" as Bacchus
Parade floats pass. The parade's theme is "Pirates of the
Caribbean."

                    ALAIN
Now this is more like it. Forget
all that cemetery business. There's
plenty of time to meet your maker.

> In the mean time, lesse l' bon ton
> rouler!

Einstein, Baxter, Forrest, Alain and the students catch
throws off the parade floats. Jonas and Einstein are not
really into catching beads. Baxter is being a good sport by
catching one or two. Gabriella catches quite a few, being
quite a looker.

After a beat the last float passes by. People mill about,
excited about their long bead throws and dubloons.

> FORREST
> Sam, I gots a most brilliant idear.
> This is a parade, right?
> Let's show Mr. Einstein here what
> we New Orleanians call <u>fun</u>.

SMASH CUT TO:

EXT. BUS, NAPOLEON STREET, UPTOWN, NEW ORLEANS, LA (1998) --
DAY

Jake the Snake's SONG "Dat's Mardi Gras" plays while Sam
drives the bus down Napoleon Street after the last Bacchus
parade float. Einstein, Baxter, Forrest, Alain and the
students have joined the parade--unofficially. The keg is
atop the bus, and Forrest has his arm around it like it's a
long-lost girlfriend while Alain, Gabriella, Jonas, Eamonn
and Lei throw beads to revelers below.

Sam yells AD LIB "Happy Mardi Gras!" out the driver's window,
while Einstein and Baxter throw beads from the bus' doorway-
-Baxter rather enthusiastically, Einstein less so.

EXT. ACME OYSTER HOUSE, FRENCH QUARTER, NEW ORLEANS, LA
(1998) -- NIGHT (ESTABLISHING SHOT)

INT. ACME OYSTER HOUSE, FRENCH QUARTER, NEW ORLEANS, LA
(1998) -- NIGHT

                    FORREST
               (popping a fried oyster)
          I bet all them Tulane co-eds
          enjoyed that ride we gave 'em from
          St. Charles Street to the Quarter
          here.

                    ALAIN
               (sipping a mint julep)
          We musta had near eighty women on
          that damn bus a yours, Sam.

                    SAM
               (smug)
          That was quite fun, huh...

                    GABRIELLA
          Sam-uel, need I remind you you're
          taken?

                    FORREST
          Speakin' a taken, you shoulda taken
          down that blonde's phone number,
          Sam.

                    GABRIELLA
               (playfully; the only girl
                present)
          Gentlemen, do you mind?

                    EINSTEIN
          We shall take a walking tour of the
          French Quarter tonight after

dinner. I would relish seeing how
the architecture has been preserved
over the years.

              ALAIN
We can do that, yessir.

              EINSTEIN
Then tomorrow we shall head back
to Cambridge.

              SAM
     (almost choking on the
      beer he's drinking)
You gotta be joking! We've got an
experience to chronicle here!
Beer, food, parades, loose women
with no shirts nor morals to boot,
culture, music--

              ALAIN
Shit yes. Lucky Dogs, too!

              SAM
Damn straight. We've got to spend
at least one more day.

              ALAIN
Well, the Rex and Zulu Parades are
tomorrow, you know.

              JONAS
     (eagerly)
Let's see the Zulu Parade.

              FORREST
Thought that would inspire you to
stay, your bein' from South Africa
an' all.

                    EINSTEIN
All right. We shall stay one more
day. But after that, we return to
Cambridge.

The group continues to eat. Sam is racking his brain
pondering ways to extend the trip. After all, he <u>does</u> need
fodder for his manuscript.

                    SAM
Bingo! Got it! Einstein, you said
you communicate with U.F.O.s
through telepathy, right?

                    EINSTEIN
That is accurate.

                    SAM
Well, after the Zulu Parade
tomorrow we're gonna continue on to
the International U.F.O. Museum and
Research Center in Roswell, New
Mexico.

                    LEI
That sounds quite fascinating.

                    SAM
Study the phenomenon at its source.
Agent Baxter, you can tell us about
U.F.O.s too.

                    BAXTER
Can't tell you anything. What's
classified is classified. I can't
stop you from finding out what's in
print or on video, but I can't tell
you anything not otherwise
available. You want to ask

Einstein, fine. But count me out.
Could lose my job doin' that.

     SAM
Okay, we strike a bargain, Einstein.
After the Zulu Parade we hit the
road for Roswell. We see the
museum. They must have a gift shop
where we can buy books. Maybe we
can even talk to the research
center's director too.

     EINSTEIN
   (resigned)
Fine...

     SAM
Okay, then, it's a deal.

     EAMONN
The adventure continues!

DISSOLVE TO:

EXT. ZULU PARADE, ST. CHARLES STREET, UPTOWN, NEW ORLEANS,
LA (1998) -- DAY

Forrest, Alain, Baxter, Einstein and the students are on
the sidewalk with a predominantly working-class African
American crowd. People scream and holler loudly for beads, a
trace more unruly than the predominantly white crowd at the
Bacchus Parade.

After a beat Alain pulls Forrest aside.

                    ALAIN
               (sotto voce)
          We're the only white folks here.
          Shit, take off your Rolex 'fore
          someone spears you for it.

                    FORREST
               (sotto voce)
          In case a riot breaks out, you
          bring any hush darkies?

They both laugh. Jonas glances over at them, wondering
what they're whispering about, then returns to watching the
parade.

Parade floats continue by. Jonas has learned through
observation of the other revelers and yells "Throw me
somethin', mister! Throw me somethin', mister!..."

A krewe member notices Jonas wearing an African National
Congress T-shirt with Nelson Mandela on it and a black "X"
cap, from the movie "X" by Spike Lee about Malcolm X.

                    KREWE MEMBER
          Where you from, boy?!

> JONAS
> From the Alexandra Township near
> Johannesburg, mister!

> KREWE MEMBER
> Well then!
>   (retrieving a purple and
>   gold painted coconut)
> Here's a Zulu coconut, for someone
> from the land of the Zulus!

People in the crowd make a grab at this coconut, but they're not gettin' it away from a very determined Jonas, who snatches it and clutches it next to his chest for dear life. This is the Hope Diamond of Mardi Gras parade souvenirs. Gabriella and the other students are shoved aside in the melee. Jonas bears a shit-eatin' grin.

> FORREST
> Looks like you made a friend there,
> Jonas.

> JONAS
> I shall treasure this always!

DISSOLVE TO:

EXT. BUS, INTERSTATE 10 WEST ONRAMP, NEW ORLEANS, LA (1998) -- DUSK

J. Loria's SONG "If Ever I Cease to Love" plays as the bus pulls onto the freeway, leaving the Big Easy for Roswell.

INT. BUS, INTERSTATE 10 WEST, LA (1998) -- NIGHT

> SAM
> It's too bad Forrest and Alain
> didn't want to come. They would've
> learned quite a bit.

                    LEI
It is apparent they love a good
time far too much to care...

                    BAXTER
It'll take us a day and a half to
get to Roswell. We'll have to ask
directions when we get there to
find the Museum.

                    EAMONN
Bloody hell. This is going to be
so cool. Imagine what we'll learn
about the U.F.O. phenomenon.

                    BAXTER
Remember, I'm mum on the issue.
It's up to you all to study the
phenomenon and ask Einstein
questions about stuff you don't
know.

                    SAM
Yeah, we know. Any more beer in
the keg?

                    EAMONN
Stark empty.

                    SAM
Damn.

                    BAXTER
Concentrate on your driving, laddy.

                    GABRIELLA
          (raising a handful of long
           beads)
Well, to New Orleans!

                    JONAS
          And to the International U.F.O.
          Museum!

                    SAM
          And Research Center!
               (beat)
          When we get there, we've got to be
          able to talk to the research
          center's director.

                    GABRIELLA
          And in a day and a half we shall.

EXT. GAS STATION, ROSWELL, NM (1998) -- MORNING

Einstein, Baxter and the students are in the gas station's
convenience store. Gabriella notes a list near the women's
bathroom.

CLOSE ON list: "Sightseeing in Roswell: 1) Library 2) Town
Hall 3) Roswell High School--Home of the Casmonauts! 4)
Police Station."

Gabriella returns to the group, which is buying morning
snacks and coffee.

                    GABRIELLA
          According to a list by the women's
          room of sights to see in town, the
          police station is an attraction
          here in Roswell. <u>Ugh</u>!

There are Asteroids and Space Invaders arcade video games
near the tables where folks sit, read the paper, drink coffee
and chat. Several WHITE OLD-TIMER MALES are seated at a
table chitter-chattering.

                    EAMONN
              (engrossed in a game of
               Space Invaders)
          Gabriella, you got another quarter?

EXT. BUS, MAIN STREET, ROSWELL, NM (1998) -- DAY

The bus makes a right hand turn onto Main Street and drives
down it. In the distance on the right is the International
U.F.O. Museum and Research Center, with a big faux U.F.O.
crashed into the side of this former movie-theater-turned-
museum.

In the distance the bus pulls into the loading zone in front
of the Museum.

INT. MUSEUM, U.F.O. MUSEUM AND RESEARCH CENTER, ROSWELL, NM
(1998) -- DAY

Einstein, Baxter and the students look around the museum
exhibits a beat.

                    SAM
          Look, it's apparent the museum's a
          waste of time. It's all, "U.F.O.s
          are cuddly, U.F.O.s are our
          friends." We need to get to the
          truth of why they're a classified
          phenomenon. Let's hit the
          bookstore and see what we can find.

INT. BOOKSTORE, U.F.O. MUSEUM AND RESEARCH CENTER, ROSWELL,
NM (1998) -- DAY

Patrick Duffy's SONG "Pickup Man" is heard from an antiquated
radio on the counter's edge near the cash register. An
ELDERLY SALES LADY with multiple piercings in her ears and
a tatoo near the top of her boobs--quite the antiquated
hipster--is behind the counter.

                    SAM
         Uh, excuse me, can you recommend
         which are the best books, pamphlets
         and videos to buy in the store?

                    SALES LADY
         Certainly.

She steps around the counter and walks over to the aisles.

                    SALES LADY (CONT'D)
         You want Robert O. Dean's
         video...The Philadelphia
         Experiment...Stanton Friedman's
         pamphlets...Bob Lazar's video
         regarding Area Fifty-one...
              (to Sam)
         You know, if you really want to
         learn about U.F.O.s you really must
         visit the library.

                    SAM
         You have a library here?!

                    SALES LADY
         Of course. We have over five
         hundred books and about a hundred
         fifty videos.

                    SAM
              (quickly handing her his
               credit card)
         Here!
              (to the group)
         Guess what?! They've got a library
         here! We're in business!

The students cheer.

INT. LIBRARY, U.F.O. MUSEUM AND RESEARCH CENTER, ROSWELL, NM
(1998) -- DAY

The students crowd uncomfortably close around the REFERENCE
LIBRARIAN at her desk, eager to begin the hunt.

> SAM
> We're looking for the best books
> and videos on the U.F.O.
> phenomenon.

> REFERENCE LIBRARIAN
> Well, I'm here to help. But you
> really should begin your search by
> browsing.

> JONAS
> But you have over five hundred
> books.

> REFERENCE LIBRARIAN
> Well, let me narrow that search for
> you all. You want to start with
> Tesla and the turn of the Twentieth
> Century. Then dive into World War
> Two and Nazi Germany. Then examine
> the Roswell crash and videos from
> the Post-war Era. Finally, you
> should examine all titles, which
> you all can do since there are so
> many of you, to find additional
> inspiration.

> SAM
> (to the students)
> Okay. You heard the lady.
> Everyone take a section of the
> library. We'll do the books first,
> then tackle the videos. You heard

her say what to look for. When you
choose a book, ask Einstein if it's
worth reading.
        (to Einstein)
Einstein, examine the table of
contents and the index to see if
the book has pertinent information
or is just fluff-stuff, like
U.F.O.s are our friends.

                    EAMONN
        Okay, let's get a-hoppin'.

TIME MONTAGE:

The students scamper around the library to MUSIC, checking
in with Einstein and sitting down to read books.

The students then watch videos.

They're dressed in different clothes as each day passes.

INT. LIBRARY, U.F.O. MUSEUM AND RESEARCH CENTER, ROSWELL, NM
(1998) -- DAY

                    SAM
        Okay, we've been here three days.
        Let's summarize what we've learned.
        Jonas, we'll use your Dictaphone to
        record our summary.

                    GABRIELLA
        Humanity's been under surveillance
        by U.F.O.s since the dawn of time.
        They've been watching us because
        they learn from us how to conduct
        their civilizations and what not to
        do. What is the best of humanity,
        they learn from. What is the

worst, such as rape or war or
violence, they avoid. They live a
communist lifestyle. No money.

Gabriella winces at this: no <u>money</u>?

> GABRIELLA (CONT'D)
> They are subject to mind control.
> This prevents crime and wars. They
> live a peaceful coexistence.

> JONAS
> They have communicated with agents
> for human change through the
> millenniums. They communicated the
> laws of how humanity should live to
> Jesus. They communicated with
> Nostradamus, as did Phase Three of
> the Phoenix Project, operated at
> Fort Hero, Montauk Point, Long
> Island, New York, by John von
> Neumann of Manhattan Project fame
> and by Al Bielek of Harvard--

> EAMONN
> Yay Harvard!

> JONAS
> --and his brother Duncan. This was
> a time travel experiment conducted
> from Nineteen Seventy-three to
> Nineteen Eighty-three. The Project
> traveled into the past, and to the
> end of civilization on the planet
> earth, including visiting U.F.O.s
> on other planets to see what
> humanity could learn from their
> civilizations.

                    LEI
Around Nineteen Hundred, U.F.O.s
began actively helping select
individuals by providing them with
inspiration for technology. Tesla
was one such example. Then in the
Nineteen Thirties, evil U.F.O.s
initiated contact with the Nazis and
Hitler. They provided technology
in return for sperm and eggs from
Germans. The Germans made a deal
with these evil U.F.O.s: genetic
Aryan material--sperm and eggs--for
civilian and military technology.

                    EAMONN
U.F.O.s reproduce through cloning.
Thus they eventually had recessive
genes in their gene pool, including
poor digestive tracts. They were
fascinated with the monkey on the
planet earth, and engaged in an
experiment: to see if they could
take the lowly primate, infuse it
with the soul of a U.F.O., including
the ability to know God, and time-
travel far into the future so as to
one day obtain sperm and eggs so they
could save their genetically dying
civilization.

                    SAM
So evil U.F.O.s first communicated
with the Nazis. The deal was:
eliminate the quote-unquote
"inferior races" and eventually
have U.F.O.s and Germans
communicate with each other on a
societal-wide basis, not merely a

governmental-wide basis. When the
Allies won World War Two, German
U.F.O.-related technology was
transferred to the United States
and to Russia, along with German
military, engineering and medical
specialists.

>   GABRIELLA
> That was Project Paperclip in
> America. The Roswell crash took
> place because U.F.O.s wanted to
> warn America about the dangers of
> nuclear arsenal, which is how they
> got into trouble in their own
> civilizations. Their technology is
> so advanced--millions of years
> ahead of Earth's--that they have no
> choice but be pacifists and
> coexist. War is simply not an option;
> they'd annihilate each other.

>   JONAS
> Surveillance and military contact
> continues to this day. The hope in
> the future is that one day there
> will be civilian contact with
> U.F.O.s That is, that U.F.O.s will
> be able to visit humanity regularly
> and we will be able to visit their
> planets regularly, the same way
> they now secretly visit our planet.

>   EAMONN
> This explains all the U.F.O.
> sightings. Then there's
> Extraterrestrial Biological Entity
> One, the first U.F.O. to
> communicate with the American

government. It said that its
civilization had reached the end.
No disease, no war, no money,
communism--in short, nothing to
live for. Life was boring, and its
civilization had lost its will to
live. They wished they were
more...human. And that's why they
want human genetic material in
their bodies. Because they must
start their civilization all over
again.

          SAM

Phew!
   (beat)
Okay, that's the essence of the
U.F.O. phenomenon, the basics. Now
let's go introduce Einstein to the
Research Center's director.

INT. OFFICE OF RESEARCH CENTER'S DIRECTOR, U.F.O. MUSUEM AND
RESEARCH CENTER, ROSWELL, NM (1998) -- DAY

The DIRECTOR is a with-it middle-aged female wearing yuppie
glasses. Einstein, Baxter and the students stand around her
office as she sits at her desk taking notes, then looking up.

          DIRECTOR
There are reasons today why the
phenomenon is still classified, and
likely will be for another hundred
years or so. After that time, we
stand a real chance of eventually
having societal-wide contact with
U.F.O.s.

          EAMONN

Cool!

DIRECTOR

Keep in mind the Extraterrestrial
Biological Entity One lesson you
learned, though. U.F.O.s are
jealous of humanity precisely
because we're <u>human</u>. That is to
say, we love life on this planet.
In general, we don't want to die.
U.F.O.s are living death.

EINSTEIN

Precisely.

DIRECTOR

With a communist lifestyle in which
there's no work, there's no
emphasis on self-actualization and
intellectual growth. They've
reached the end. Humanity is just
at the journey's beginning. If we
had contact with U.F.O.s before we
were prepared as a planet for it,
people would expect U.F.O.s to
solve all our problems, to answer
the truth about God and religion.
It would destroy human civilization
the same way the white man with
superior technology destroyed
Native American civilization.
Besides, if U.F.O.s solved all
humanity's problems, what would
humans do all day if there were no
need to work?

EINSTEIN

Do you have any questions for me?

DIRECTOR
Lord, a million, I suppose.
Questions about religion, time-
travel, and humanity's future.

EINSTEIN
Well, I shall inform you about all
that.

GABRIELLA
I have a question. What ever
became of Adolf Hitler after he fled
to a compound outside Buenos Aires?
I read about his escaping
to Argentina as part of the Odessa
File in one of the books.

DIRECTOR
Well, when humans die, they are
reincarnated into babies' bodies.
U.F.O.s oversee this phenomenon.
Sometimes you get lucky. You are
reincarnated into the Trump family.
Other times you're unlucky. You
get reincarnated into a starving
family in Africa only to die of
AIDS.

GABRIELLA
So Hitler's soul was reincarnated?

DIRECTOR
So were the souls of Bormann,
Kammler, Mueller and the rest of
the Nazis. Everyone gets
reincarnated. You should study
Buddhism and read Conversations
with God, Volumes One through
Three, by Neale Donald Walsh.

                    LEI
What if you communicate with
U.F.O.s as the Nazis did? Can you
select a desirable family in the
next life if you work with U.F.O.s
to arrange this?

                    DIRECTOR
I don't see why not.

Gabriella looks at Sam uncomfortably. She's beginning to
sense something's up...

                    DIRECTOR (CONT'D)
Well, everyone, I'd like to talk
with Mr. Einstein and Agent Baxter
in private about classified
matters. Agent Baxter, you can
tell Einstein not to answer any
question you deem fit. Lady and
gentlemen, will you excuse us?

INT. HALLWAY, RESEARCH CENTER, U.F.O. MUSEUM AND RESEARCH
CENTER, ROSWELL, NM (1998) -- DAY

The students stand around a water cooler talking.

                    GABRIELLA
Sam, this is serious. You're from
an elite German-American family
living in America and you're
Nostradamus' Third Antichrist.
That qualifies you as the
antichrist predicted in the Bible.

                    SAM
Look, Gabby, I know. It's not an
attack on religion. It's
specifically an attack on the

Pope's position regarding "Be
fruitful and multiply." We're
gonna have four hundred million
people in America and fourteen
billion people on this planet in
the next forty years or less.

                    GABRIELLA
That's not what I'm getting at.
Hitler didn't die in a bunker. The
Germans came to America in Project
Paperclip and to South America in
the Odessa File. The American
government was communicating with
U.F.O.s. They had the potential to
reincarnate themselves into elite
families.

                    SAM
So what're you getting at?

                    GABRIELLA
          (bluntly)
Sam, take two guesses who you were
in a former life.

INT. BUS, INTERSTATE 10 EAST, TX (1998) -- NIGHT

It's snowing. The oversize windshield wipers are flapping
back and forth loudly. Everyone is silent a beat.

                    SAM
Einstein, Agent Baxter, why didn't
you tell me?

                    EINSTEIN
You weren't ready for the truth.
How do you think I would feel if I
had caused fifty million to die in

a former life? That I tortured millions of Jews and other types of peoples thought to be inferiors? I made the choice to come to Nineteen Ninety-eight to help you and humanity because it is at a crossroads not with nuclear weaponry but with regards to overpopulation and environmental degradation.

> SAM

So now what? Hitler solved the problem of lebensraum with killing people in World War Two. Today we have no wars. We have global peace. How do you stop the Pope from preaching no birth control? How do you tell people to only have two children at most, and if they want more to adopt?

> EINSTEIN

You must learn to lead. You care only for being famous and making money off the name of being the antichrist. Instead, you must learn to serve. You have plenty of family money. You <u>will</u> be famous. That is a given. However, you <u>must</u> learn to serve.

> SAM

Christ... When we get back to Cambridge I better have a meeting with Reverend Gomes of Memorial Church in Harvard Yard. Ask him what to do.

INT. REVEREND GOMES' OFFICE, SPARKS HOUSE, CAMBRIDGE, MA
(1998) -- DAY

REVEREND PETER GOMES, a roly-poly bespectacled African
American preacher with a baritone voice, sits behind his desk
as Sam sits in a chair in front of it.

              SAM
So now we know the truth about God.
That it's an all-knowing amorphous
entity that created the universe
and let it run through evolution.
What do I do now?

              GOMES
My advice is tell no one. Let that
which God is remain a mystery. Let
life remain a mystery. You know
what every C.I.A. agent knows, what
Mr. Einstein knows, but you don't
see them talking, now, do you? No,
my friend, let life remain a
mystery.

              SAM
That's it? Shut up about it?

              GOMES
Now, you could ruin the secret, but
why...? No, it is fine to speak
out against the Pope's stance on
not giving countenance to birth
control, but don't attack the Roman
Catholic Church. A great many
people believe in that religion,
and to them it is sacred ground.

                    SAM
What's the point of knowing all
this if I can't talk about any of
it?

                    GOMES
I'm afeared that is for you to
determine for yourself. Talk with
Mr. Einstein. You may also talk
with me at any time if you become
confused and lose your way. But
always remember, my friend: that
which is sacred must remain so.

INT. LIVING ROOM, HOUSE, DANA STREET, CAMBRIDGE, MA (1998)
-- NIGHT

Einstein, Baxter and the students are seated about the
living room.

                    SAM
Okay, my turn to speak, Agent
Baxter.
Here's what we've determined: that
I'm Hitler reincarnated. We have
to go back in time to that compound
in Argentina where Hitler was
living before he died and talk with
him.

                    BAXTER
And precisely what're you gonna ask
Hitler? That you're him? You
already know you are, and he knew
you are too.

                    SAM
Look, I'm him in a future life. I
have a future life too, in some

other body. So does everyone in
this room. Because I'm him
reincarnated, we know reincarnation
exists. We know if it can happen
once, as it did to me, then it's
possible for it to happen to
everyone. Here's what that means:
not only am I reincarnated, but Eva
Braun, my former wife, was
reincarnated too.

        BAXTER
So you wanna know who Eva Braun is
today?

        SAM
Yeah.

        BAXTER
  (softly)
It isn't me, is it?

        BAXTER (CONT'D)
No, it ain't you.
  (beat)
Look, Gabriella, you're dating Sam
here 'cause he's rich and 'cause
you all in this house responded to
the same advertisement for a house
in Harvard Square for rent. I
gotta hand it to you all, this is a
mini United Nations here. But no,
Gabriella, you don't marry Sam.
The person he marries is Eva Braun
reincarnated in a new life.

        GABRIELLA
Shit...
  (arising and leaving)

I'll be in my room.

          BAXTER
Look: yeah, I do have the ability
to get you all back in time to see
Hitler, but I wanna explain
something to you. Eva Braun is the
Hollywood actress Laura Harmann,
the Jewish Gen X bombshell.

          SAM
<u>She</u> was my wife in a former life?

          BAXTER
Yeah, and let me tell you what else is
strange. She's gonna be your
wife in this lifetime as well. So
now I'm like Marty McFly. I have
the ability to introduce you to her
through C.I.A. connections to get
you married to her. But here's the
deal. She's loving, she's
spiritual, and she's sensitive.
You, you're a nerd, you're greedy, and
you're not mature enough for
her. Yeah, she's a comedian. But
she's also got a serious side. And
she doesn't want to be married to a
jackass. Buddy boy, you got some
serious growin' up to do.

          SAM
Get me to Laura Harmann. We'll
have her accompany all of us to see
Hitler in that Argentine compound.

          BAXTER
Christ. The shit this job
requires...

                                              DISSOLVE TO:

INT. POLO LOUNGE, BEVERLY HILLS HOTEL, BEVERLY HILLS, CA
(1998) -- DAY

Einstein and Sam arrive at the Polo Lounge's maitre d'
station. LAURA HARMANN sits at a table alone in the
distance, anticipating these two.

                    SAM
          Einstein, how do I look?

                    EINSTEIN
          I care not a wit for
          superficialities. Neither I'm sure
          does Ms. Harmann.

                    SAM
          She's a top-ranked Hollywood
          actress.
               (pointing)
          Look at her. She's a most fine
          physical specimen.
               (beat, straightening tie)
          Well, so am I, I suppose...

                    EINSTEIN
          Be yourself.
               (beat)
          Come. Accost, Sir Andrew, accost.

Einstein and Sam approach the table at which Laura Harmann
is seated.

                    SAM
          Laura, thanks for agreeing to meet
          with us. I'm Sam Hamm, and this,
          this here's Albert Einstein.

Sam and Einstein take seats at the table. Laura pinches
Einstein softly.

                    LAURA
          Wow, the Real McCoy.

                    SAM
          As I'm sure the C.I.A. told your
          agent, we have kind of a unique
          situation on our hands. I'm in the
          process of writing a novel about
          Einstein here time-traveling at the
          K-School--

                    LAURA
          K-School?

                    SAM
          Oh, the, uh, Kennedy School of
          Government at Harvard.

                    LAURA
          What does the Kennedy School
          specialize in? Politics?

                    SAM
          Yeah. Anyway, uh... This is going
          to be really hard to tell you, and to
          be honest, I don't know how to
          do it. That's why, uh, I brought
          Mr. Einstein here to meet with you
          and me.
               (beat)
          Einstein, you tell her.

                    EINSTEIN
          You tell your future wife.

                SAM
Einsteeein,
        (sotto voce)
Shuuut uuup, you're unkinding the
ride here.
        (beat)
Listen, <u>you</u> tell her. Only don't
tell her <u>that</u>.

                EINSTEIN
That she's your future bride?

                SAM
Eiinsteeein... <u>Please</u>.

                LAURA
        (pleasantly)
Will one of you two please tell me?

                EINSTEIN/SAM
        (pointing at each other)
He will!

                EINSTEIN
I shall say nothing further until
you speak first, Samuel.

                SAM
Oh boy... Here goes... Uh, Laura,
it's like this, see. I'm
Nostradamus' Third Antichrist.

                LAURA
What?! I was led to believe I was
just meeting Einstein and a friend
of his!

> SAM

And it gets even weirder.
Nostradamus' Third Antichrist is
the same antichrist predicted in
the Bible.

> LAURA

So it's your job to speak out
against God...

> SAM

Well, no. God does exist, because
Einstein here communicates with God
through telepathy.
> (beat)
And he communicates with U.F.O.s
too. But anyway, it's my job
specifically to speak out against
the Pope preaching against birth
control, because the population of
this planet is on its way to
fourteen billion people and four
hundred million in America.

> LAURA

Oh. And I thought my job was
hard...

> SAM

Yeah, well, I'm sure it is. Being
a top-ranked actress and all. But
anyway, the C.I.A. has offered to
have Einstein, my friends at the K-
School and me go back in time to
Nineteen Sixty-seven to meet Adolf
Hitler in a compound outside Buenos
Aires, and well, we need to borrow
you to do this.

                    LAURA
          (flatly)
You <u>do</u> realize I'm Jewish.

                    SAM
Yeah, and so is Einstein here. But
there's a reason why we need you
especially.

                    LAURA
And what would that reason be?

                    SAM
You see--this here's the hard part
to explain...
          (long beat, breathes
           deeply, exhales)
You're Eva Braun reincarnated.

                    LAURA
<u>What</u>?! She was German, she was a
Nazi, and she was Hitler's wife!

                    SAM
Exactly.

                    LAURA
So if I'm Eva Braun reincarnated,
who were <u>you</u> in a former life?

                    SAM
Okay, Einstein, I spoke first.
Now's your turn.

                    EINSTEIN
What we have here, Ms. Harmann, is
a unique situation. All people are
reincarnated when they die. Should
you not believe me, research

Buddhism, as taught by His Holiness
The Dalai Lama. One's soul never
dies. It simply reinhabits
different bodies in different
lifetimes indefinitely.

        SAM

Uh, yeah. The book Conversations
with God by Neale Donald Walsh
describes this.
    (beat)
And since you're doing such a great
job at explaining this, why don't
you keep going.

        EINSTEIN

You see, this gentleman before you
was Adolf Hitler in his former
life. And you were his wife, Eva
Braun.

        LAURA

Shit!...

        EINSTEIN

Adolf Hitler's soul was
reincarnated into an elite German
family in America--

        SAM

Nice elite German family. I'm
not like Napoleon and Hitler,
Laura. I'm the nice antichrist.

        LAURA

Jesus, what is this, an
advertisement for Seven-Up?!

                    EINSTEIN
Yes, a nice German-American family.

                    LAURA
Okay.
     (beat)
This is a <u>little</u> hard to believe.
But I'm trying.
     (in better spirits)
This is a lot to lay on a lady the
first time you meet her. I <u>can</u>
understand all this. I suppose.
Buy why do you need <u>me</u>?

                    EINSTEIN
Your future husband and you are
going to travel back in time with
me and his Harvard friends to meet
Adolf Hitler.

                    LAURA
     (pointing to Sam)
And <u>you're</u> my future husband?

                    SAM
Einsteeein...
     (softly, pleadingly)
Help...

                    LAURA
     (smiling)
Well, you <u>are</u> kinda cute... But
what on earth is a young Jew going
to say to Hitler?

                    EINSTEIN
This is why we are here.

                                        DISSOLVE TO:

EXT. FORT HERO, MONTAUK POINT, LONG ISLAND, NY (1998) --
NIGHT

SUPER: "FORT HERO, MONTAUK POINT, LONG ISLAND, NEW YORK"

A black van with tinted windows pulls up to the gate.
MARINES in uniform talk with the VAN'S DRIVER a beat to
check identification papers, and then wave the van through.

EXT. FORT HERO, MONTAUK POINT, LONG ISLAND, NY (1998) --
NIGHT

The van pulls up to a nondescript brick building. The van's
doors open, and out comes Einstein, Baxter, Laura, Sam, and
the students. JOHN VON NEUMANN and AL BIELEK approach.

                    VON NEUMANN
                (shaking hands)
            Albert, good to see you. And you
            must be Sam I Hamm.

                    SAM
                (shaking hands)
            Hi there. Who are you?

                    VON NEUMANN
            John von Neumann, formerly of the
            Manhattan Project. And this is Al
            Bielek, who works with me on Phase
            Four of the Phoenix Project, which
            this time traveling project is.

Everyone shakes hands as Baxter AD LIB introduces Laura and
the students to von Neumann and Bieliek.

                    VON NEUMANN (CONT'D)
            Here's the deal. We're sending you
            all to the year Nineteen Sixty-
            seven. Adolf Hitler has been

informed by the C.I.A. you all are
coming. Einstein, you and Ms.
Harmann here's safety is assured.
Marines will be present as you all
speak. Take as much time as need be
with Hitler, and take careful notes
for your book.
    (smiling)
Can hardly wait to read this one!
    (beat)
Anyway, once you are done meeting
with Hitler, you will be
transported back to today. You
will only be gone a minute in
Nineteen Ninety-eight time. In
Nineteen Sixty-seven you will have
as much time as you require.

                    SAM
And I thought my girlfriend in high
school got around. Einstein, you
get around more than Amtrak!

                    BIELIEK
Okay, we're ready to send you all
back in time. Come with me.

EXT. SAN RAMON COMPOUND, BARILOCHE, ARGENTINA (1967) -- DAY

A U.S.A. Marines truck with Einstein, Baxter, Laura, Sam and
the students pulls up to a compound's gate. It's guarded
by ARGENTINE SOLDIERS. After the TRUCK'S DRIVER shows
identification papers, the truck enters the compound.

EXT. PATIO, SAN RAMON COMPOUND, BARILOCHE, ARGENTINA (1967)
-- DAY

Einstein, Baxter, Laura, Sam and the students stand ready
to be introduced to an aged ADOLF HITLER--he's one step away

from the grave--by an ARGENTINE SOLDIER. Hitler sits in a patio chair in the distance, and there are eight chairs near him in anticipation of his guests. The Argentine soldier approaches Hitler.

                    SOLDIER
          Sir, you are here.

                    HITLER
             (beat, looking at him,
              brusquely)
          I know that.

                    SOLDIER
          No, I mean, you in your future life
          are here. Samuel Hamm from America
          is here with Evan Braun, now named
          Laura Harmann.

                    HITLER
          Those C.I.A. rats! How dare they
          make Eva a Jew in her next life!

                    SOLDIER
          However, you are to be a <u>rich</u>
          German American.

Silence. Well, at least he'll have spending money--and therefore assured power--in his next life.

                    SOLDIER (CONT'D)
          Furthermore, Albert Einstein is
          here.

                    HITLER
          I should have had the S.S.
          assassinate that jew-boy on the spot
          back in 'Thirty-three before he and
          all

those Jew scientists could flee to
America!

Laura winces in the distance. <u>This</u> was her former husband?

                    SOLDIER
          He is protected by American
          Marines. They are here to see you
          with students from around the world
          from Harvard University in America.

Silence.

                    SOLDIER (CONT'D)
          Shall I send them forward?

Hitler waves his hand around. Bring them forth. The soldier
approaches the group.

                    SOLDIER (CONT'D)
          Adolf Hitler will now see you all.

                    LAURA
          Swell.
               (sotto voce)
          Hi, honey, I'm home. How was your
          day?...

The group members approach and all take seats. Sam and
Laura sit next to each other. Einstein sits next to Sam
on his opposite side. Baxter and the students take the
remaining seats.

                    SAM
               (trying to smile
                cheerfully)
          Well, uh, let the games begin.
               (beat)

Uh, I'm you. And you're me. See,
I'm you reincarnated. And this,
this is your wife, Eva Braun.

Hitler clearly does not approve of all this.

                    SAM (CONT'D)
What we have here is a unique
situation. You see, you ruled
during World War Two during a time
of overpopulation.

                    HITLER
          (gruffly)
Lebensraum.

                    EINSTEIN
          (to the students)
That is German for "elbow room" and
the need for it.

                    SAM
Your solution was to cooperate with
evil U.F.O.s to have Germans become
the chosen race to take over the
planet earth by killing off quote-
unquote "inferior races." This
would have included Einstein here,
and Laura Harmann, your wife
reincarnated.

                    EINSTEIN
The world at the turn of the
century rapidly faces a similar
situation. It is overpopulated
and is becoming environmentally
degraded.

                    GABRIELLA
At current growth trends it will
reach fourteen billion people on
the planet earth by Two Thousand
Fifty.

                    SAM
However, know this. Human
evolution has been accelerated.
When you look at us around the
table here, you see we are better
looking, taller, smarter, healthier
and will live longer than previous
generations.

                    HITLER
What do you think Joesef Mengele
was working on in the concentration
camps?! We were working to create
you all! A master German race, as
it has been in ancient times in
Atlantis on the planet earth long
before recorded civilization.
People think civilization began
with the Egyptians. Hah! It
began eons ago with Lemuria and Mu
and Atlantis! Then those Aryans
overpopulated the planet, and a
cataclysm was created by U.F.O.s.
The U.F.O.s thus started from
scratch, and it took human
evolution a long time to build up a
civilization again.

                    BAXTER
The Central Intelligence Agency in
America is working with U.F.O.s as
we speak. We're accelerating human

evolution for <u>all</u> humanity, not
just Germans.

>   HITLER
>   (gruffly)
> You do that because you have
> civilians from all countries living
> in America who become citizens.

>   JONAS
>   (indignantly)
> Including blacks.

>   LAURA
>   (softly)
> And Jews.

>   HITLER
> You listen to me now! We did the
> best we could with what we had in
> the time period in which we did it.
> U.F.O.s saw humanity as insects to be
> killed. Germans were intellectual,
> good looking, cultured, patriotic.
> We had destiny before us. The rest
> of the world was inferior. If we
> were so wrong, why did U.F.O.s come
> to <u>us</u>?!

>   EINSTEIN
> They came to you National
> Socialists because you all were as
> evil as them. Other U.F.O.s, like
> the Pleiadians, who are kind and
> benevolent, communicated with the
> American government to hold the
> evil U.F.O.s at bay. But by then
> it was too late. You had advanced
> military technology from them, and

World War Two was subsequently
fought.

              LAURA
And six million Jews died in the
concentration camps and over
fifty million died in World War
Two. Those Jews were starved to
death and tortured because of <u>you</u>!

              HITLER
You listen to me, girl!
International Jewish bankers were
threatening to take over the world!
They were threatening Germany! You
are an American now, Eva.

              LAURA
<u>Laura</u>.

              HITLER
       (growing fanatical)
Read Henry Ford's <u>The International</u>
<u>Jew</u>! Read <u>The Protocols of the</u>
<u>Elders of Zion</u>! Jewish bankers
threatened Germany! They
threatened <u>my</u> country!
       (beat)
And <u>my</u> people!
       (beat)
It is a leader's job to lead the
masses. People need to be led.
You didn't live through what I did.
The overpopulation. The threat
of Jewish bankers bankrupting my
country. You have no idea what
patriotism is. And, you have no
idea what power lay before us with
our communication with U.F.O.s.

BAXTER

We picked up where you left off.
Germans came to America after World
War Two to help us face off against
the Russians in the Cold War. We
wanted Germany's military and
civilian technology. And what we
were able to do by communicating
with U.F.O.s is to continue to
advance human evolution.

HITLER

You say I'm wrong for what I did,
girl?! You listen to him!

LAURA

But Americans did it humanely! The
entire world has benefited, not
just Germans!

HITLER

And thankfully not just Jewish
bankers, either!

LAURA

How dare you speak that way to a
Jew!

HITLER
   (calmly)
Eva, you always were a plaything.
You never did understand. I
married you for intimacy, but
certainly not for your brains.

LAURA

You listen up, you! Today I'm a
top-ranked Hollywood actress, and I
am proud to say I'm an icon of my

generation, called Generation X!
And I'll tell you something else!
We Jews are leaders in Hollywood!
Know why?! We learned from you!
We said if we could control
the message being shown in movies,
we could shape this world into
a better place! And you know
something, we have!

                HITLER
Eva, you amaze me. You finally
learned to think.
        (beat)
You are smart in your new body. I
must congratulate you. But someone
explain to me why you had to be
reincarnated as a Jew?

                BAXTER
I'll explain. It was an experiment
with U.F.O.s to see if we could get
a rich German to marry a Jew born
into poverty, a Jew who would
become a top-ranked actress.

                HITLER
And this is the result, what I see
before me? Her?
        (pointing to Sam)
And him?

                BAXTER
After the end of World War Two, a
time-travel experiment was
conducted based on a time-travel
experiment done by you all, the
National Socialists.

HITLER

Yes, we were time-traveling.
Bormann, Kammler and Mueller were
responsible for that. They
reported directly to me. We
traveled into the past. To the
time of Jesus Christ. And to
ancient times of Atlantis, Lemuria
and Mu. There we discovered
Germans were the Chosen People, not
by God, but by U.F.O.s because they
wanted to reincarnate themselves
into Aryan bodies.

BAXTER

Right. Well, America conducted our
own time-travel experiment. This
time it was led by the folks who
worked on the Manhattan Project
that was responsible for developing
the atomic bombs dropped on Japan.

HITLER

We had that technology first. We
gave you that technology in return
for guarantee of safe passage of
Germans to America after World
War Two. You in America made the
decision to drop nuclear bombs on
Japan to win the war. Then you
agreed not only to rebuild the
German economy for our cooperating
with you as the war drew to a close
but also to rebuild the Japanese
economy as a way of apologizing to
them for the use of the bombs.

                    BAXTER
What we're looking to do now is to
colonize the moon and Mars to deal
with overpopulation on earth. It's
called Alternative Three.

                    HITLER
You've been communicating with the
Russians to do this ever since the
end of World War Two. It is about
humanity's survival should the planet
earth become environmentally
degraded and uninhabitable.

                    EINSTEIN
Your solution was to line people up
and shoot them in wars to prevent
overpopulation. In Nineteen Ninety-
eight there is peace around the
world. Nations no longer fight
each other, they cooperate.

                    HITLER
          (to Jonas)
So niggers are equal to Germans?!

                    JONAS
How dare you!

                    HITLER
          (looking at Laura)
And Jews are equal as well?

                    LEI
          (proudly)
And China is on its way toward
becoming a superpower.

GABRIELLA
And the Brazilian rainforest is
becoming endangered from
deforestation for lumber. And in the
favelas overpopulation caused
by a lack of birth control and a
lack of education is rife. Without
an education, people have nothing to
live for.

LAURA
That is the lesson Jews can teach
the world. Education comes first.

HITLER
You people have benefited from the
sacrifices and hard work of those
who gave their all to make the
Twenty-first Century possible.
        (to Baxter)
You bring me Albert Einstein.
        (to Einstein)
All you did all day Mister Albert
Einstein was think! I actually
did!

EINSTEIN
It was how I thought, and what I
thought about, and my
communications with God and U.F.O.s
That will help solve Twenty-first
Century problems.

HITLER
And it was my hard work getting rid
of insects of human life that
cleared the path for future
generations of more-evolved beings

like yourselves to inhabit the
planet. You boy,
    (pointing to Jonas)
you can't tell me that every nigger
on the continent of Africa looks
exactly as you and is as smart as
you. You are a Harvard boy. A
chosen one. Africa is destitute
and overridden with human life.

    JONAS
Africa has problems, yes, but we
shall overcome them with time.

    HITLER
And you, from China, you reproduce
like rabbits, and you are poor.

    LEI
We have a one child policy now, and
Chinese are among the hardest
working and smartest people in the
world.

    HITLER
And you, boy, where are you from?

    EAMONN
    (proudly)
Belfast, Northern Ireland.

    HITLER
Are you Protestant or Catholic?

    EAMONN
    (fearing the worst)
Catholic.

HITLER
And the Irish don't practice birth
control and drink excessively and
are lazy and stupid. Yes, yes, you
too are a Harvard boy, indeed a
chosen one too, but look at the
mess and waste of population that
is Ireland. Beautiful countryside,
but a waste of a population.

EAMONN
Today Ireland is a part of the
European Union, and today we have
benefited from good jobs and
economic growth precisely because
we have the lowest cost of doing
business in Western Europe.

HITLER
(pointing to Sam)
This leaves you. Or should I say,
me.

HITLER
What of this Jew you are dating?

SAM
Well, I was dating her,
(pointing to Gabriella)
and now, well, I don't know who I'm
dating.

HITLER
You, girl,
(pointing at Laura)
Are you going to marry him?

> LAURA
>
> I just met him. I don't really
> know anything about him.

> HITLER
>
> My advice, boy, marry a rich German
> who will respect you and honor you,
> not a Jew who only wants you for
> your money.

> LAURA
>
> Hey! I have plenty of my own
> money! I'm a successful Hollywood
> actress! Don't you dare tell him
> not to marry me! Look, I'll show
> you, you bastard--maybe he and I
> will get married, and live happily
> ever after! How do you like them
> apples, fuckhead!

Silence.

> HITLER
>   (calmly)
> Twenty years ago, if you had said
> that to me, I'd of shot you between
> the eyes, girl.
>   (beat)
> Ladies and gentlemen, I shall
> retire for a nap.
>   (rising to leave)
> Good day.

Hitler stares a beat at Laura, then Einstein, then at Jonas, then finally at Sam and leaves, accompanied by that Argentine soldier. Laura looks over at Sam. This is what he was in a former life? And now, is this thing she just saw going to become her future husband in a reincarnated body?...

                    SAM
Einstein, what now?

                    EINSTEIN
Now we will write out your
manuscript and your speech that you
will present at Harvard in December
Nineteen Ninety-nine. You usher in
the new millennium. And Laura, you
shall help write it.

                    BAXTER
Come, let's get going. Let's head
back to the future.

INT. SAM HAMM'S BEDROOM, HOUSE, DANA STREET, CAMBRIDGE, MA
(1998) -- NIGHT

Sam, Einstein and Laura are scribbling away, drafting what
is obviously a speech. Einstein and Laura make corrections,
describing AD LIB what they think should be included. And,
Einstein is telling him some ideas to exclude. The rough
draft manuscript of the book Sam will write sits nearby on
the desk, at least a thousand pages.

Finally, all three stop writing and take a breath or relief.
The speech is finished.

                    EINSTEIN
All right, this is your speech you
will present in December Nineteen
Ninety-nine. Quite good, I must
say. You've learned much over the
course of four months.
        (pointing to manuscript)
There's your manuscript,
        (gesturing to speech)
and here's your speech. You do
realize what this means?

                    SAM
              (sadly)
          Time for you to head back to
          Nineteen Forty-eight, huh?

                    EINSTEIN
          Precisely. However, I can time
          travel, you know. Perhaps I'll
          check up on you in the year Two
          Thousand Thirty. You may be
          Secretary General of the United
          Nations by then, or President of
          the United States. And yes, Ms.
          Harmann, that would make you First
          Lady if you were to marry Sam.

                    SAM
          Einstein... Pleeease...

                    LAURA
              (giggling)
          Who knows what the future holds...

Einstein stands, and exits Sam's bedroom for the living room.

INT. LIVING ROOM, HOUSE, DANA STREET, CAMBRIDGE, MA (1998)
-- NIGHT

Einstein approaches Baxter, who's reading a book on Hitler.

                    EINSTEIN
          Agent Baxter, it is time. The
          speech is complete. Time for me to
          head back to Princeton.

                    JONAS
              (seated, looking up from a
              book)
          You're <u>leaving</u>?

                    EINSTEIN
My work here is complete. It is
time for me to return to the past.
Besides, I have work to do there.
I have to work with my colleagues
at the Institute for Advanced Study
at molding the Post-war Era so that
this moment in time can happen.
It's not just about even today,
with the turn of the millennium
fast approaching, it's about the
future as well.

Lei enters and sees a serious conversation underway.

                    LEI
What is going on?

                    JONAS
          (dejected)
Einstein's leaving.

INT. LIVING ROOM, HOUSE, DANA STREET, CAMBRIDGE, MA (1998)
-- NIGHT

Everyone is gathered in the living room. Sam and Laura
stand next to each other, and Gabriella is seated next to
Jonas and Lei.

                    BAXTER
Einstein and me, we leave tomorrow.
I've arranged for a car to take us
back to Montauk Point where I'll take
him back to the year Nineteen Forty-
eight.

                    EAMONN
What then becomes of you?

                    BAXTER
Well, I go to work on a different
assignment. That's the way it goes
in my profession. I'm like a
global handyman. I go from
assignment to assignment where I'm
needed.

                    GABRIELLA
We'll miss you, Einstein.

                    LEI
We now know the past, present and
future because of you.

                    JONAS
And I have learned there is hope
for all blacks in Africa.

                    GABRIELLA
And the poor in Brazil.

                    EAMONN
And we have peace in Northern
Ireland today because people like
you and Gandhi and Martin Luther
King and Nelson Mandela showed the
path toward cooperation from
conflict.

                    EINSTEIN
You are a good people around the
world today. But you have much
work ahead of you if you are to
prevent overpopulation and
environmental degradation.

                    LAURA
              (sprightly)

> Sam's gonna knock 'em dead at
> Harvard in a year from now! And,
> I'll see to it that he appears in a
> movie or two. Who knows, I bet I
> can even have his book become a
> movie!

        SAM
> We gotta get over a thousand pages
> down to the size of a book, and
> then down to the size of a
> screenplay.

        LAURA
> If they can do it for Mario Puzo's
> The Godfather, they can do it for
> your work too!

        SAM
> I vote we celebrate. To Mr.
> Bartley's!

        GABRIELLA/JONAS/LEI/EAMONN
> To Mr. Bartley's!

        LAURA
> Who's Mr. Bartley?

EXT. MR. BARTLEY'S HAMBURGER COTTAGE, HARVARD SQUARE,
CAMBRIDGE, MA (1998) -- NIGHT (ESTABLISHING SHOT)

INT. MR. BARTLEY'S HAMBURGER COTTAGE, HARVARD SQUARE,
CAMBRIDGE, MA (1998) -- NIGHT

'Sixties MUSIC plays from speakers in the restaurant as the
group laughs and talks loudly AD LIB with burgers and shakes
before them as they sit at a table near a poster of Albert
Einstein. Sam eats a French fry with ketchup on it and gets
ketchup on his cheek. Laura wipes the ketchup off his cheek

with a napkin. The camera PANS around the restaurant to
see the funky posters, including the signs that read "Main
Street" and "Hollywood." MR. BARTLEY walks past and asks if
they need anything.

INT. STADIUM, HARVARD UNIVERSITY, CAMBRIDGE, MA (1999) --
DAY

SUPER: "HARVARD UNIVERSITY, DECEMBER 1999."

Sam is at a podium, dressed in an expensive Italian suit.
He appears very professional, very much a leader. He's
changed from the nerd he's always been to the future leader
he will become.

                    SAM
          ...And so, as we look toward the
          coming millennium, we do so with
          prosperity and hope, but also with
          warning and much work ahead. For
          the spiritual, it will be a golden
          age. However, this must be coupled
          with pragmatism. It is the longevity
          of humanity that is sacred, not
          every sperm and egg. For those who
          preach against birth control, the
          Twenty-first Century will be one of
          conflict between them and those who do
          practice birth control. And we do
          know this. Now is the time to seize
          that which ages before ours have
          struggled for. Now is the time to
          set goals for having a one-world
          government and for setting future
          generations up for societal-wide
          contact with U.F.O.s. Let us make
          it a goal to have such within a
          hundred years. And, let us have
          the goal of colonizing the moon and

Mars and having human beings living
on these planets within a hundred
years. And on the planet earth, let
us have as a goal environmentalism
that preserves the planet for future
generations.
Yes, there is much work ahead. But
we know this. Where God walks, so
walks humanity. I am Samuel Hamm,
and I am your antichrist. Thank
you, God bless, and good afternoon.

The crowd uproariously applauds. This has been his finest
hour thusfar in life. Laura rises from her seat next to
Reverend Gomes and Harvard President LAWRENCE SUMMERS and
approaches Sam. She kisses him on the cheek, and they hug.
The Twenty-first Century is in good hands.

THE END.